In the Garden Where We've Been Planted

In the Garden Where We've Been Planted

Oliver Yardley

Bibliologica Press

Acknowledgments

This story was inspired by Joseph Conrad's novella *Heart of Darkness* (1902), which acted as the wellspring for adaptation. Extracts from the 1969 song *Where Do You Go to (My Lovely)* are used with the kind permission of the estate of the late-Peter Sarstedt.

ISBN 978-0-6485093-2-5

First published in 2018 by
Champagne Book Group
Albany, Oregon, USA

This 2020 revised edition by
Bibliologica Press
Unley, South Australia, 5061
Australia

A catalogue record for this book is available from the National Library of Australia

Dedication

To Ann, who captured the heart of this American man.

One

There were cracks in the sidewalk that caught the fallen leaves. The cracks looked like little fingers reaching out to snatch the brittle structures as the wind blew them to some imaginary destination. The sun made this otherwise unremarkable scene something of a marvel, especially because of the way the light was diffused through the red leaves still hanging from the tree.

At that moment, I thought that people were like trees. Some were planted in gardens that allowed them to grow and thrive, while others could only strike their roots wherever the wind blew their seeds. The winds of fortune blew hot and cold, so it was the luck of the draw whether the seeds would prosper. I looked up again. The sun was playing a hide-and-seek game behind the sparsely covered branches.

I thought, *Even the Garden of Eden wasn't a paradise.* If I had believed in God, I would've been angry to think that a Divine Power purposefully set out to incorporate hardship into Life's design. But knowing that life was about random variation—happenstance, fluke, luck, quirk—not deities, I could accept these anomalies. We are all dealt a hand of cards at birth, and it is up to us to play that hand at the Table-of-Life the best we can. It's the limits of the cards we hold—and good luck or misfortune—that determines our prospects. We simply need to learn how to flourish in the garden where we've been planted.

Then, as if it were off in the distance, I made out Miles Stoner's gruff voice. But his words were just garbled sounds. The joy of watching the prismatic colours of the leaves as they danced with the sun was far more rewarding than listening to the monologue of a dour, self-righteous man, but he managed to divert my attention.

Stoner was middle-aged with a stomach that hung over his belt, causing his shirt to be untucked. He held a camera almost parallel with the sidewalk. In his unmannered way, he said, "See, if you take the picture from this angle it shows the height of the crack. If you take it looking down, you lose the depth of field; it looks flat." He paused and stared at me as if I was a mental incompetent. "And we don't want it looking flat in court. We want it to look like Mount Greylock. We want the judge to see why the plaintiff tripped."

His arm jutted out, pressing the camera against my chest. "Here, shoot a few frames and let me see 'em." He pushed the camera at me harder—it was an expensive Nikon digital single-lens reflex.

I held it but dared not to look up because my impulse was to drive the camera into his face and tell him to look at it from that angle.

"Okay," I said, staring at the camera, "leave it with me, I'll practise." I managed a smirk, but not a smile.

"Good attitude. I like you." He didn't, and I knew it, but I didn't care. "You'll develop well," Stoner said, then walked back into the building.

I stood thinking, *Who the hell does he think he is?* I didn't need lessons on how to photograph the gap between two slabs of concrete. More importantly, I thought I had lost direction, and like the winds of fortune, I was being blown into the cracks along with the dead leaves. I was coming to the view that joining this agency was a bad decision. I should have never sold my PI business after my wife's passing. But before I could decide whether I should smash his SLR on the sidewalk and apologise for my 'clumsiness,' or do as I was told, my cell phone chimed. I fished it from my backpack.

2

It was a Boston number, but one I didn't recognise. I retrieved the voice message and heard a woman's voice. In a flat tone, she said, "This is Yvette Kerslake. I need to speak to you. My number is..." and then rattled off a series of numbers.

Her name didn't mean anything to me at first, but then I recalled reading about some controversial art exhibit she curated at a museum several months back. Something to do with American Indian art. This was a relief because I sometimes got calls from people who were convinced, they were being followed by secret government agents or were having their thoughts stolen by the Illuminati's supercomputers. This woman, however, sounded normal.

I put the phone in my backpack and returned to the office where I left the camera on Stoner's desk—he was at the coffee machine cooking up another latte. Waving to him, I said, "Got to go."

"Okay," he replied. "Do you think you'll master the art of macrophotography?"

I gave him the thumbs-up, controlling an urge to show him my middle finger and to tell him to sit on it. I walked back out the door and onto the street.

Two

My jeep was parked around the corner on Maple Street. East Longmeadow was one of a few small towns in Western Massachusetts that didn't have a Main Street. Maple Street was it's *de facto*.

As I walked, I phoned Sophie, my eldest child, to see if she had finished work for the week and wanted a ride home instead of walking. She said she'd appreciate that, so I made my way over to the medical clinic where she worked in the lab while she studied for her doctorate in medicine. I needed to talk about my future, and Sophie was a good sounding board. As Ellen slipped away, Sophie was the bravest of my three kids during those six months. Despite radiation and chemo, there had been no hope. Sophie saw it in herself to take over as the family's matriarch.

The Stoner camera incident had been the latest put-down from the newly appointed lead investigator. I thought taking a contract job with this agency was a way to soothe the pain of Ellen's passing. Didn't work out that way. The relief never came, and it only postponed facing up to the fact that I lost my life's companion. Seeing that tree today made me realize I needed to adapt to this new garden.

I pulled into the clinic's parking lot and saw Sophie waiting in front of the neighboring building, Romito's Italian Delicatessen. She was talking with her friend Rose Kozynski, who worked at the deli.

"Thank God it's Friday," Sophie said as she got into the passenger's seat, slamming the door.

I didn't reply. As an atheist, I never could work out whom to thank for Fridays. I waved to Rose, and she came over.

My arm rested on the doorframe of the open window, and she placed her hands on it. She leaned forward to talk. It was the first time we'd touched. We had met for coffee a half-dozen times over the past year when our paths happened to cross at the supermarket. She was funny, bright, and had a positive attitude. Rose wasn't stunning, but she was good company. She had a warm smile and a gentle laugh.

Rose was my age. I got the sense she'd be interested in getting to know me better. She had lost her husband a few years before Ellen's death. He'd been a factory foreman, who was killed in an industrial_accident. Rose was demure, not one for bars, clubs, or Internet dating. I don't think she saw many men in the years since her husband died.

I wasn't sure I was ready, but when she touched me, I realized the time had come. Tired of living alone, I wanted to spend my future with someone. I wanted a warm and trusting relationship, a relationship that flourished in good times as well as whenever the world served up the pain it held in reserve. What I missed the most since Ellen's passing was the comfort of being held in a woman's arms. The sensation that a woman's body provides in the face of the day's worries was soothing. I would have enjoyed that now.

As she and Sophie said their goodbyes, I couldn't help daydreaming about Rose touching me. I tried to absorb the tingle it infused in me. I wanted to store the emotion in a reservoir, so I could call on it later. I didn't want to drive away.

Rose smiled, squeezed my arm, and said, "Hey, I'll see you soon?"

I couldn't let her go. Without thinking, I blurted out, "Listen, the cinema is showing re-runs of a few of the classics. They're screening *The Maltese Falcon* on Monday night. What say we go?"

As the words passed my lips, I cringed at the awkwardness of my suggestion. What a stupid thing to say. I hadn't asked a woman on a date since before I married. Wasn't sure if that was how it was done, but I didn't know when I'd run into her again.

She hesitated, looked down. "Oh, I have something on Monday." She lifted her gaze. "Let's do it another time."

"Sure, no problem." I drove off feeling foolish and rejected. Being older, asking for a date should be easy, but there was the same self-doubt and hurt I had when I was young. *Another time?* Was that a polite way of saying, 'don't ask again', or was it genuine? Had I misread the signs about her interest in me, or was I being too sensitive?

As my jeep gained speed along the deserted road, I turned to Sophie and asked, "What was that about?"

"Well, if you were going to ask Rosie out, you waited too long! The two of you would have had so much fun together. She started seeing that guy from Dillon Realtors, Michael Drew. They're going to that movie on Monday. She told me a few days ago." Sophie folded her arms and stared forward.

I couldn't accept that Michael Drew was seeing her. He was one of those slick salesman types with the ability to embellish anything, including his public image. Time waits for no one, and I'd waited a year. Was I experiencing a twinge of jealousy, or was it envy?

"She's planning one of those fourteen-day European tours." Her eyes met mine. "Soon," Sophie said, as if to imply, 'Move fast, or you'll be left behind'.

Hmm? A European tour? That would be one long coffee conversation.

I flinched. *Drew couldn't be in the mix for that. Surely not.*

Sophie gazed out the window. "So, how was it?"

"Do you mean work?" I asked. "If that's what you mean, I've had better days." I turned the wheel hard to the left, heading up the hill out of town.

She must have sensed my frustration. She was good in that way. "Why do you let him get to you? He probably thinks you're after his job."

"I'm not after his job. If I wanted to be the boss again, I would have applied for it when it was advertised. Anyway, you flatter him by crediting that halfwit with enough brains to actually think."

There was a moment's silence. All that was audible was the whirr of the motor and vibration of the deep-tread tires.

"I want to ask you something," I said,

"You want to get serious about Rose?"

I smiled. "I have been thinking about it."

"She's nice, isn't she? You know, being sentimental is charming, but dwelling on the past won't bring Mom back. It'll only ensure you'll miss out on a new love."

Her acceptance provided respite to my taxed emotions having been robbed of my wife's companionship. Hearing those words meant I could relax, get on with enjoying life after years of long hours at work. I could start to see a place in my mind's eye for Rose Kozynski in my future. I had to think of something to head off Michael Drew. I needed a strategy.

"Do you think there's hope for someone new in my life?"

"Yes, but you have to take a chance." She glared at me as if to underscore her point. As if scolding a disobedient child, she waited for my response.

I swallowed hard. "Okay, I'll take a chance."

"You have to let go. Inertia is disastrous when it comes to love. Bertrand Russell said, 'Of all forms of caution, caution in love is perhaps the most fatal to true happiness'." She glanced at my smartphone on its dash holder. "Why's your phone flashing?"

"Oh, it's a work message."

Immediately Sophie had the phone on loudspeaker, acting as my secretary, retrieving the voice mail, and making note of the number on a pad.

"Strange, it's a 617-area code. Is that Boston? Do you know this woman?" She paused then said, "Why would she want you to phone her?"

"Potential client I suppose. Never met her, but remember her name being associated with some museum in Boston. A controversial person from what I've read."

I pulled over to the side of the road. I enjoyed sitting in the car at the top of the hill at the end of our street. From there I can see across the valley to the peaks in the distance. At that time of day, when the sun was setting over the hills, it reflected the warmth of whatever was left in the autumn sun. The leaves had turned various colors that made them glow orange. Spellbinding.

"Dad why are you stopping here?"

"The colors. I like the colors. They help me remember."

"Remember what?"

"Not sure." I paused for effect. "It's obviously not working."

Then with the long drawn out inflection that only a young woman can do, she said, "I hate when you do that. I thought you were serious. You act the same as a teenager. Are you ever going to grow up?"

At twenty-three, Sophie was practical, though she still had quite an appreciation for emotional matters, especially when compared to her fraternal twin sister. She was the sensitive one of my children.

She turned away then back at me. I knew it wouldn't take long for her to soften.

"Then again, I'm not sure I want you any different." She smiled. "I love you."

"I love you, too," I said. I lied. Not about loving her, I did. I lied about the colors. I did remember when I saw them and recalled the autumn I noticed them for the first time. It wasn't that I didn't until that year, but it was in the year I met Ellen. We were in a second-hand bookshop in Northampton. She was a post-doc student at Mount Holyoke College, teaching anthropology. Listening to her Scottish accent, while she paid for her purchase, was captivating. Later, her intellect proved seductive.

As I started the engine, Sophie asked, "Are you going to call Yvette Kerslake? She'll be getting annoyed you haven't returned her call."

Sophie would be a tough boss. "I'll phone her after dinner."

"I'll tell you what, seeing as it's Friday night, you phone her when we get home, and I'll cook. How's that for a deal?"

I turned the jeep onto the road, but immediately saw a car approaching. I waited. It was a black BMW with tinted windows. A man drove by with a woman half his age in the passenger's seat. Michael Drew. I fought back a groan. Seeing him flitting around with whatever woman took his eye, confirmed my disgust.

"Dad, you okay? What are you staring at?"

I wanted to say, *I'm trying to imagine Drew with a personality*. Sophie hadn't seen him, so I made an excuse. "Oh, it was something I need to remember to do at work on Monday."

I drove down our long crushed-stone driveway. Ellen had chosen the material to remind her of her childhood house in Scotland. Over the years, I came to enjoy the ambience of the pebbled path. At the house, I turned into the parking apron in front of the garage, pressed the remote to open the door, and drove in. The phone call now lay ahead.

* * *

My personal library was in the den. I headed there, while Sophie went to the kitchen. The book-lined walls provided comfort and security. I loved reading. Over the years I had built up a fine collection. I often recalled the words of the poet, Joseph Brodsky, who said, 'There are worse crimes than burning books. One of them is not reading them.' In some ways I saw myself in the mold of P.D. James' Adam Dalgliesh, a bibliophile detective.

I picked up the desk phone and dialed. It rang, and I heard Yvette Kerslake's voice. I introduced myself and apologized for missing her call then listened to what was on her mind.

She told me she was a curator at the Boston Museum of Fine Art. She oversaw the American Indian collection. Then, she blurted out, "I need your help." Her voice sounded as if she might have been crying. *I'm not sure if it's sorrow or despair.*

"I need you to conduct some private inquires for me. Can you come here so we can talk? I need to keep this low key." She spoke *sotto voce*, almost as if her hushed tones would keep people from finding out we had spoken.

A job outside the firm? That wasn't done. Management frowned on PIs moonlighting. Yet I was intrigued by who she was and wondered what it was about. I said, "Sure, when?"

"As soon as you can. Do you have...a free appointment tomorrow? In the morning, please?"

That was Saturday. I was off, but my schedule was full of personal tasks. "Yes, I'm free tomorrow morning." She started to tell me her address, but I interjected with one of my PI jokes. "I know where you live, I'm a detective."

10

It was meant as a bit of humor, but she said, "Oh yes, of course, I should have realized. I'll see you at ten, if that's okay," and rang off.

I sat holding the handset then slowly replaced it into its cradle. I didn't know what to think. One thing was for sure, she was in no mood for comedy. I now needed to find where she lived so I could uphold whatever super-sleuth image I might have created.

I went online and checked the *White Pages* listing for her name. It's what intelligence analysts call 'open-source information.' And there it was. I was saved from the embarrassment of having to phone her back. While online, I searched newspaper archives for articles about her. There were a few, one with a picture. She was impressively dressed.

"Well, what did she say?" Sophie's voice came from the kitchen. "Were you eavesdropping?"

"I'm the daughter of a private investigator. What would make you think anything of the sort?"

"Is dinner ready?"

"Pour yourself a drink and tell me what she said."

There was a bottle of Glenmorangie single malt in the dining room cabinet. I poured a sizable amount into a glass then sat at the kitchen table, while Sophie finished up. Coming from Scotland, Ellen always had a bottle in the house to remind of her life 'back home.' I maintained her tradition. I had a swallow, and the alcohol's therapeutic effect warmed my throat.

"First, tell me about your day," I said.

The burning sensation of the whiskey became more enjoyable with each sip. I knew in a few minutes that, on an empty stomach, I'd experience the drink's full pleasurable effects. I suspected that Sophie thought so too, and that's why she suggested it.

As she spoke, I held the bottle of Glenmorangie and read the distiller's description of the spirit on the back label. It said, "...alluring and very complex..." It made me reflect on the picture I saw of Yvette Kerslake on the Internet and her call for help. *Our meeting in the morning should be interesting.*

Three

I stood viewing the photograph that sat on the fireplace's mantelshelf. A studio portrait, not some holiday snapshot akin to the ones I stuck to the side of my refrigerator. It had an antique, gold-gilt frame. Everything about the photo exuded privilege. This was underscored by the pearls Yvette wore. Not faux. All her adornments appeared expensive.

I examined Yvette Kerslake's husband more closely. He was standing next to her, had wide-set coal-black eyes, thick eyebrows, a stumpy nose, and no smile. He wore aviator-style glasses that went out of fashion with button-fly jeans. The lenses were so thick they deformed his eyes. Perhaps he thought he was starting a new retro something-or-other trend. Hard to tell with artists if this type of thing replicated their view of art or were simply in bad taste. Anyway, my guess was that when the cards for good looks were being dealt, he wasn't sitting at the table.

Poor guy. What could she have seen in him? It was certainly something other than physical attraction.

Yvette Kerslake's house may have been an indication. A big two-story place with an attic, located in Lincoln, one of Boston's more prestigious suburbs. *This didn't come cheap.* Gauging from the other houses in the neighborhood, I guessed the median family income had to be more than four times that of the average taxpayer.

The tall brick home had gables, the roof in the left front corner sloping down over what must have been a sitting room for welcoming guests. On the right, about midway along, was a double set of windows in what was the formal dining room, the top half lined with stained glass patterns. The driveway led to a small set of outbuildings. One had the hallmarks of being a servant's quarters, and the other, a more modern, all-glass design, an art studio. There was a virgin white Mercedes-Benz C180 parked in the driveway. The license plate read HER-180.

Clearly, she enjoyed the treats that money brought. I imagined that included travel, meeting important people, and a career others could only dream of.

Had her husband provided the cash to fund all this? I planned to find out.

Turning back to face her sitting on the leather Chesterfield in the living room, I probed, "So tell me about how you and Kurt met. I'm guessing it was through the Boston Museum of Fine Art. The American Indian collection? I remember seeing your photo in the newspaper when you opened the exhibit that raised a storm of controversy." I didn't tell her I found that information last night on the Internet.

"Kurt is a descendant of the Narragansett tribe. His artwork has a large following of admirers. He's well respected and gets glowing reviews. His works sell well. He's a remarkable man."

"Is that what attracted you to him?"

"What do you mean?" she asked tersely.

"Hey, I'm not the one who's suddenly gone missing. He is, and I need to know a lot of background if I'm going to find him." I moved to the sofa opposite her and sat.

"Why?" she shot back.

She was certainly not used to being questioned. This was a woman who would have only one gear in her car—overdrive.

I took in a breath, "Because people are people, and although they change *where* they live, they find it hard to change *how* they live. If I take on your case, I need to understand who he is and how he thinks. That'll give me a better chance of finding him. Besides, how do I know this isn't a police matter, foul play, an accident, or something else the cops will take a dim view of if I intervene without telling them?"

"No police." Her gaze was pained, voice flat but direct.

Her body language told me she didn't tolerate being corrected. She was not only a woman who lived well but needed to be in charge. This was going to be a problem if I decided to take on her case. The management of investigations was my domain, and *I* needed to be in charge. *What's this all about?* I pushed for answers.

"Okay, let's start with the basics. What's his full name?" I started jotting notes into a small coil-bound pad.

"Kurt Kerslake."

"Does he have a middle name?"

"No middle name."

"Other names he's used over the years? Nicknames shortened names, that sort of thing?"

"No, only Kurt. You can't shorten it beyond that."

"Okay, but what about a 'stage name' or whatever artists have? Was he adopted, had another name at birth?"

She crossed her arms. "No."

"Hey, if you don't give me the facts, I may decide not to take on your case. I need this information to track him down." *With two names it's going to be difficult to make a positive ID. Then again, it could be worse, as he could have had only one name, like Tarzan.*

"What do you mean, take on the case?" Her expression hard, voice indignant. "I thought you had. That's why you are here isn't it?"

"No, I am here to hear you out. You called asking for help. I know nothing of the situation surrounding his disappearance, so how could I decide to find him?" I let that sink in. "Besides, he's not missing. Only socks go missing. So, we're not going to find him in the laundry basket, at the bottom of a drawer, or with the last cycle of washing. He knows where he is, and I suspect others do too. We don't, and there's a reason for that. He doesn't want us to know. I need to know why." With some degree of ambivalence, I asked, "Does he have a girlfriend?"

She glared and snapped, "No. Certainly, not!"

Unless there's proof, either way, experience has taught me such things aren't that certain. "I'll be blunt—how do I know he didn't leave because you were dishing out a pile of emotional abuse? Contrary to popular belief, many men suffer at the hands of their wives—shame, embarrassment, and other fears. There's no way I'm finding him if that's the case. I'm going to have to know more, so can we continue." I took in a quick breath. "Otherwise, I'll go."

Her jaw clenched. Her lips pursed.

I stood and started to walk out.

As I got to the door, she called out, "No, wait!"

I turned, locked her in my stare. Her green eyes were sending a message contrary to her indignation—one of anguish.

She had striking features: chestnut-brown hair, soft olive skin, full lips, and long shapely legs. Tall at five feet ten, and thin, she had a smooth, model-like cleavage. She could have worn anything and still looked good, either an evening dress or casual slacks. The omen on the whiskey bottle last night was proving true. She was certainly alluring, but more importantly, very complex.

Clearly uncomfortable with the situation, she shifted in her seat. The sofa made the low rumble that well-oiled, well-worn leather does. Her eyes appeared as if they were about to well with tears. *Perhaps I was too harsh?*

I suspected she wouldn't be receptive if I tried to break-the-ice with any of my lame PI jokes.

She said, "I want you to take on the case because I need all this to be confidential." Then she winced. "I don't want people finding out he left."

"Why me? There are dozens of private investigators in the Boston area who are more than capable of finding him—more so than me since it's not my current specialty. I've done all sorts of investigations, but now I recover stolen manuscripts and rare edition books for insurance companies. There's a big difference." I wasn't about to tell her that since selling my PI business, I was demoted to photographing cracks in sidewalks...

"That's true, but I don't know the others or their reputations. I know you. I mean, know *of* you. I understand you recovered the Roger Williams text for a gallery in Hartford."

"Yeah, didn't he set-up a settlement for Indians in some part of Rhode Island?"

She frowned. "A shameful event."

"Sorry?"

"His settlement was attacked in autumn of 1675 by Colonialists. The result was the Great Swamp Massacre. Over 500 killed. Mostly elderly, women, and children. It was the Narragansett tribe's winter camp."

The fact she knew of my book recovery surprised me, as did her interjection about the book's subject.

She went on, "Not quite an accurate discourse of what took place, but an important artefact nonetheless. You were discreet in that matter, so I know you'll treat my inquiry confidentially. Anyway, you have a reputation for success. The recovered manuscript is a testament. I only found out because I'm a close friend of the gallery's owner."

I had a flush of mixed emotions. I was flattered that she thought highly of my work, but my thoughts were beginning to drift into the shadows of what she was saying. I was uneasy. *No one to know? Discreet?* Her words ran through my head like dried tumbleweeds rolling down the street of an abandoned frontier town.

I needed time to think, so I said, "Okay, let's start over. Make me a coffee."

Her shoulders dropped their defensive posture. I watched her breathing slow and deepen. "Fine, I should have offered you a drink when you arrived. I was anxious to get things moving."

Yes, single-minded and driven.

"Do you want something stronger?"

"Much too early for Scotch. Coffee will be fine."

Yvette Kerslake turned to the door leading to the passageway and called out, "Isabel, please prepare coffee for two." She asked me, "How do you take it?" There was now warmth in her voice and her smile. Her watery eyes became more composed.

"Black, strong. No sugar," I said.

I wondered why a man would leave her. It didn't make sense, to have her so concerned for his well-being and all the trappings of success, yet leave, simply disappear? I wanted to find out.

Isabel González, her housekeeper, entered the room holding a silver tray containing a pot of coffee, milk, and sugar. She was an older woman who could have easily been a grandmother. There were also two fine china cups, silver spoons, and Czech crystal water glasses.

"Thank you, I'll pour," Yvette said as Isabel placed the tray on the table between us.

18

Isabel tried to set the tray down but experienced some awkwardness, perhaps arthritis. As I listened to the exchange between her and Yvette, I realized Isabel was a native of South American, probably from Venezuela, a country with a less than stellar record when it came to human rights. Despite all the trimmings of wealth, Yvette appeared to have liberal leanings.

I suspected her comment about the rare book subject suggested she supported other left-of-center causes. I took her employing this South American woman as another indicator.

I watched Yvette pour, and her hands—their color, texture, and shape—were in marked contrast to her housekeeper's. There were no spots or blemishes. She had no scars that were common for people who clean and do manual tasks. Her hands were smooth, evenly tanned, and her nails manicured. The nail polish complemented her blouse. *She lives well, and she treats herself to the luxuries life offers. Hmm, that some people's lives offer.*

Although I watched the cups being filled, my concentration moved to Yvette's face. I could see in my peripheral vision her short hair, reminiscent of the glory days of the 1920s. The bangs in front highlighted her long, angular face. Her hair was as smooth as her skin and as well presented as the rest of her.

At my age, my hair was starting to show strands of gray, but she was a few years younger than me, so her color was possibly natural. Nevertheless, that wasn't a question to ask a woman and certainly not one *this* PI was going to ask *this* woman.

She gazed out the window with the appearance of being lost in thought. She asked my rates and offered to pay me a week in advance.

"Not until I know the details," I said.

She squinted at me with her emerald eyes. "Not many people say 'no' to me."

"Listen, I need to get details."

As if she was talking to herself, she muttered, "You must be discreet."

Then, before she could explain, the housekeeper appeared at the door holding her right-hand. In an excited voice, she said, "Excuse me, miss, I am sorry, but I have injured my hand on the syringe in the trash."

Syringe? My mind became alert. *Okay, this is something I need to hear.*

Getting up to help Isabel, Yvette said matter-of-factly, "Kurt is a diabetic. He injects insulin."

This seemed odd. I assumed diabetics used pens, not needles.

I followed the two of them into the kitchen where there was a first aid kit. As Yvette attended the wound—it was deep, the needle long and thick—I poked around for information that might help me find Kurt. There wasn't much hope of having a rummage through his personal things in the bedroom, so I stuck my nose here and there without making it too obvious that's what I was doing.

When I turned to the window, I saw a clue. Stacks of empty wine bottles were piled up ready to be put out for curbside recycling. The volume of discards had a similar appearance to an adolescent's first booze party, but I guessed they were Kurt's. Things were now making sense.

"Isabel, get your coat. I'll take you to get this looked at," Yvette said. "Needle stick wounds are difficult to clean because they don't bleed freely."

When the housekeeper left the kitchen to retrieve her wrap, I pointed out the window and asked, "Kurt's?"

Her facial expression was one of resignation. She probably realized I wasn't about to give up until I had answers.

She grimaced. "Kurt's an alcoholic. Has been for years. He refused to get help, and now it's too late. He has cirrhosis and liver cancer. He's also a diabetic and has a heart condition. These are serious health issues. I need you to find him. Can you see why he needs to be home? Physically, he's quite ill."

And mentally too to be drinking that much. "I'll need a photograph of him."

She walked me back to the mantel and handed me a small framed picture that was probably taken at a theatre event.

"I'll need it without the frame, so I can scan it for the dossier."

"I want him, not the photo. I don't care what happens to it," she replied.

Cold and decisive, not romantic. I guessed she was never one to read Jane Austen. I slipped the photo out of its frame and into my folio.

As I started for the front door to let myself out, she grabbed me by the arm. "You'll go about this diplomatically?"

My mind flashed to the needle. "I'll be subtle, but I need to point out that if he is up to something illegal, there is no client-investigator privilege recognized in law. The only privilege that exists is between a lawyer and his client. That privilege can be extended to me as the investigator if you were to engage one."

She shook her head. "There'll be no need for a lawyer. I know you'll give me one-hundred percent."

"I always give one-hundred percent in everything I do, except when I give blood." My stab at humor didn't lighten her mood, so I went on, "In the meantime, message me Kurt's date of birth and social security number. Also, I need to know if he's done this before and where he might go, his usual haunts. Text me those details."

She was already making moves to take her housekeeper for medical treatment. As I closed the door, it made me reflect— PIs could move between the lowest levels of society and the upper echelons, but the transition wasn't easy. As sad as it was seeing the troubles of people 'on the street' with all their overt misery, prosperous people were equally dysfunctional. The only difference was that they wore a Rolex instead of a Timex.

Four

After I cleared the tollbooth at the entrance of the Mass Pike, I headed west, back toward East Longmeadow. I eased myself into my jeep's cushioned seat and experienced the low rumble of the tires as the vehicle picked up speed. Then my cell phone rang. I pressed the answer button on the steering wheel's hands-free control and heard Corey Granfield's eager voice. Corey was always excited. And his enthusiasm for life was infectious.

"Hey buddy, got an email from Lucian, he's back from Abu Dhabi. He'll be in town for a few days before heading off to some symposium in Norway. You free to get together tonight?"

It wasn't a question, because before I could answer, he said, "Great! We'll meet at Perotti's at seven. Pizza and beer. Shouldn't—my diet—but hey, Lucian's home."

Corey always lifted my mood. He was the classic Good Time Charlie. He loved to eat, drink, and tell stories; hence he had three times the body mass index of an athlete. I acknowledged his plan and rang off.

* * *

I arrived at the appointed hour to find Corey and Lucian Trudeau had already set themselves up on stools at the bar. They were near the entrance, joking with Giacomo Perotti, the owner. Both held brown bottles with Pabst Blue Ribbon labels.

Lucian once said he enjoyed Pabst because it reminded him of what living in the 1950s would have been like and reminiscent of those stylish couples that featured in the ads *New Yorker* magazine.

Lucian worked as a management consultant to several international businesses. He lived most of the year in the United

Arab Emirates but flew around the world regularly to speak at conferences here-and-there, mostly in Europe. His latest wife, the third, was Gjertrud, a Norwegian he met on an overseas business trip, so I suspected this conference was part of a tax deduction for them to visit her family.

He was always well-presented, and tonight was no different. He wore Italian lace-less shoes, finely woven black woolen trousers, open neck silk shirt, and a jacket tailored for him in Hong Kong. Corey was dressed like me in jeans and a sweater. We were New Englanders; our dress suited the weather.

"Hello, Jack," I said as I approached the bar.

Giacomo was in his eighties. He'd run the restaurant for decades. A family business, one of the few that survived the spread of chain-style restaurants. His daughter Micaela ran the kitchen with her husband Enrico Romani, but Jack and his wife, Elżbieta, were the *maître d's*. They knew everyone in town and made it a point to know patrons' tastes and needs.

Lucian stood and shook my hand. Corey gave me a brotherly hug.

Jack asked me, "Hey, have you heard the joke about the Swiss banker and the lawyer? Tell 'em, Corey. It's the funniest thing I've ever heard."

"I'm sure he'll tell me later," I said and gave Jack a nod.

The restaurant was a good place to catch up. Jack had the lights low, but not so dim the place had a shifty appearance. The smell of Italian sauces from the kitchen, as well as the sounds of the waiting staff as they hustled about, gave the place a welcoming atmosphere. One could sit for hours enjoying the food and the company.

Unlike my other long-time friends, when Corey, Lucian, and I got together, we didn't reminisce about the past. Those were the memories that bound us. Instead, we discussed the future.

We heard Lucian's tales of travel and the gossip of a life abroad where he moved in the circles that make the chronicles of business magazines.

Corey continually came up with new business plans to sell something or other on the Internet, which usually bordered on some form of get-rich-quick scheme. He called it *entrepreneurship*. Made me think of the timeless used car dealer anecdote, 'I'll give you less for more.'

Nevertheless, he had yet to file for bankruptcy and had sent his two children to private colleges in Connecticut.

As we walked over to our favorite booth, Corey said, "Lucian is heading back to Europe for a—what's it again? Some symposium on, what?" Before Lucian could answer, Corey continued, "Hey, never mind, it's the usual. He's still marketing his ideas on streamlining management practices we know will never happen, though management always seems to want to hear about it." He laughed and said to Lucian, "You know my offer for us to do business is always open."

Nodding toward Corey, Lucian threw his hands in the air and turned to me. "Now that you know my latest, what're you up to? Any big crime busts?"

"No busts but had an interesting call from a Boston woman about a private inquiry she wants me to make. I'm not certain I want to take on her case." Then it struck me. "Corey, you're a diabetic. What do you use to inject?"

"Disposable insulin pens. Why?"

I ignored his question. "How long are the needles on those pens?" "Oh, about a quarter inch. You worried about my diet?"

"So, a half inch needle would be used for—"

He finished my sentence, "Injecting drugs."

"Thanks." I needed to change the topic before they caught on. "I don't want you going into an insulin shock or whatever happens when you eat and drink as much as you'll do tonight."

With mock aggression, Corey punched my arm. "It's a diabetic coma. Don't worry; I split my dose, half before and half after the meal." He frowned. "Hey, you're starting to sound like Beth."

"So, is that the problem? This case is about drugs?" Lucian was faster on the uptake than Corey.

I sidestepped the question. "I'm working for an employer now, and moonlighting is tantamount to contempt. It would get me fired."

"Buddy, listen, you ran your own agency for years. I know the types of operations you did. Some were risky. Why would getting fired matter to you, especially now?"

I smiled. "I want to start a new life. Grow old."

The two of them leaned back, probably not knowing what to make of my statement. I thought about Rose and being with her. Life could be nice, comfortable, easy, fun again. I considered the option of going on that European tour.

Lucian broke the silence. "Well, you'll need money to do that. So, ask yourself, is this client paying?" He leant forward. "I'll answer that. She is, so it's commerce. Don't worry about that firm you're working for. Take on the case, do the job, bank the money. It's what we call *business.*"

"Hey, if you paid him for that advice, it would have cost you the high end of three figures," Corey laughed.

Lucian said, "Four. Granted the low end of four, but four nonetheless." The two of them chuckled.

Elżbieta walked by the table on her way to greet a newly arriving group, stopping by to say hello. She acknowledged

Lucian with a motherly kiss on the cheek—*must have been his Italian shoes*—and Corey and me with warm embraces.

I thought Elżbieta's well-timed interruption might divert the conversation, but it didn't.

"Listen, even if you don't want to imitate Amos Burke— the millionaire LA police detective who drove a Rolls-Royce— you still need dough to start this new life you're planning," Lucian reminded me.

It was typical of him to couch his advice in a chic image, but Corey could always bring the conversation back to basics. He was like a terrier with a rat.

"New life means a new woman." He raised his eyebrows, his eyes twinkling.

"Okay, I'm attracted to someone. And before I am cross- examined by you two, I'll lay out the facts, she's local, my age, you don't know her, and she's a widow. She's a nice person. Good company. Friendly. Soon, I hope she'll be more than that."

Wearing a big grin, Corey said, "Wow, sounds like *love* to me."

With my chin raised, I said, "Yep, I think so." Yet, as I said that, I wondered if it was love, or only the memory of love.

"So, when do we meet this mystery woman?" pestered Corey. "Hey, next time we should bring the girls. Good opportunity to see her."

As I studied my beer going flat, my mind returned to the Kerslake case. *Should I take on this new work right now?*

Corey told a joke about not wanting snails on his seafood pizza because he wanted *fast* food. We groaned at the punch line.

"Okay, okay, so you heard that one. Well, what about the time I bought Beth the wrong birthday present?" he asked. "She told me not to buy her anything expensive. So, I didn't. And I ended up sleeping in the guest room for the next two nights."

"There's no doubt women are smarter than men, but we still have the advantage because we're too dumb to know that," I said, excusing myself to go to the men's room.

Corey's advice about the syringe left me uneasy. The image of Kurt's needle was vivid in my mind's eye. Yvette Kerslake's devotion to finding the man who abandoned her was equally unsettling. I wanted to meet her husband and ask him what the hell he was thinking when he walked out on her.

On my way back, I passed Jack. He asked if we needed anything else. I leaned against the bar and told him we were quite comfortable. I considered his aging face, one that seemed to have wrinkled with life's experiences. "Jack, what would you say to me who's looking for a new partner?"

He smiled. "Listen, there's no life after death. All this nonsense you hear about near-death experiences only feeds the thinking of crazy people that there's another life waiting for us when we die. I think it gives them hope, the possibility for something better. That thinking takes away the beauty of living." He swept his hand across the restaurant; his gesture encompassing all the people enjoying themselves. "We need to make the best of what we've got, while we've got it. You need to love someone, experience that love for all it's worth, and help that person do the same." His eyes widened. "The remedy for a love lost is a new love. We don't get a second chance tocome back to earth." He winked. "You didn't hear that from this good Catholic. I'll never admit to saying *that* in the confessional."

In my line of business, it's not what the secret was that matters, but what you do with that information. That's what defines a PI. "Your secret is safe with me," and returned to the booth.

Corey and Lucian were imitating sharks in a feeding frenzy. The pizzas had arrived, and the smell of the rich tomato sauce, roasted green peppers, garlic, and pepperoni was overpowering. As I ate, I reflected on Jack's advice. Ellen wouldn't be back. All I had was her memory. We experienced good things. Although her life had ended, mine was going on. I daydreamt about Rose, but I questioned myself. *Was it love?*

Any affection I had for her vanished when I walked to my jeep. As I inserted the key into the ignition switch, a set of headlights crossed my car from another vehicle that had entered the parking lot. While my jeep warmed up, I noted the direction of the vehicle and saw two people getting out, heading to Perotti's. It was Drew, and the woman with him was Rose Kozynski.

If I believed in astrology, I suspect my horoscope would have started by saying, "Are you sitting down?"

Five

Monday morning didn't clear my thinking about Yvette Kerslake's case. She was being guarded about Kurt's details, only messaging me the information I asked for and nothing else. The question of what would make a man walk out on such a devoted person maintained my curiosity. I have to admit that on Sunday, my thoughts were being occupied by another challenge. I wanted to ambush Michael Drew. Of course, there was the boring work awaiting me at the agency lurking in the back of my mind.

Even so, my interest in this man without a smile was strong. As I put the coffee on to brew, I thought I'd at least conduct a basic search to see what information was out there. I started with an Internet query and was soon joined by Sophie carrying two mugs of black coffee.

"What ya doing?"

"Having a think about what the Boston case might involve."

"So, you *still* haven't made up your mind?"

"No. It's complicated."

"Can't be. Searching the Internet isn't difficult. You want my help?"

She tried to nudge me off my chair.

I resisted her shove. "Searching isn't complicated; the client's complicated. I mean, my thoughts about the client's case are complicated." She stared at me with an expression of bewilderment.

I clasped my hands. "I'm not sure I want to take on this job."

"Okay, it's all the same to me," she said and wandered back into the kitchen. The aroma of warm croissants filled the air.

I typed Kurt's name into the search engine, hoping to gauge the scale of the problem I might face. Sometimes finding a missing person was a job for more than one person.

There was no point in doing the other usual 'first steps' that the *Missing Persons Manual 101* would advocate—if there was such a handbook—such as doing a *White Pages* search because this wasn't that type of case. There was also little point in logging into any of the specialized databases available to me for skip tracing.

So, I did an Internet search as a way of assessing the size of the information universe on Kurt Kerslake. I needed to see what was out there. When doing this type of search, there were two results that bring me dread, a 'no results found for...' and an endless stream of hits. After pressing the enter key, my screen flashed with only a dozen results.

This is pleasing. There was enough information to generate some leads, but not so many I'd never be able to hunt down everyone.

As I scrolled through the entries, I mentally ticked off what Yvette texted me against what was coming up on my screen. Social media sites showed he'd been a long-time patron of a few Boston bars. I made a note of their names and addresses, and the nights he drank at them. *Might have to use a pretext and see who'll talk.*

I scrolled further, coming across a few blogs where he discussed his political views. His ramblings were on Native Americans and how the Federal Government 'stole' their land. He wrote about how there was some place no government knew about, and how indigenous peoples of the world could go there to escape oppression.

I made notes in the hope that these too might develop some leads, but I suspected that if such a place existed, the IRS would have passed a law declaring it an illegal tax haven.

I reread his statements. He didn't seem to be acting normally. *Was he drunk when he typed this, or is this some sort of fringe political view?* Sounded a bit loony. Yvette's political left leanings dovetailed with this theory. I made more notes.

There were websites and blogs about his artwork. Critics were positive in their appraisal of his paintings. There was only the odd disgruntled comment. I wasn't an art aficionado, so I couldn't evaluate the reviews, but I did recall Yvette saying his work was well received and selling. Judging from her lifestyle, it was probably true. Then again, it could have all been purchased on credit.

For a minute, I thought I should do a credit check on the Kerslakes, but Kurt's anti-government comments were more intriguing. I dismissed the critics' views. *Who am I to pass judgment on some artist's work when I like Salvador Dali?* What did Henry David Thoreau say about art? 'It's not what you look at that matters; it's what you see.'

Then I saw *it*. One of those one-in-a-thousand discoveries a PI stumbles across. Normally, PIs waste hours pounding shoe leather, or sitting endlessly in a car with a long-lensed camera, and nothing happens. It's what we call the 'all leads lead to nowhere syndrome.'

It wasn't on the main results web page. I had followed a few links to subsidiary pages where people talked about his art and political muses. I could have easily overlooked the link, but by chance, I clicked on it.

I'd found a blog by an Australian Aboriginal group in the outback. I knew from my wife's work as an anthropologist that the outback was the remote inland area of Australia, where there were either no people or so few people it didn't matter counting them. It was always a fascinating idea that a continent about the size of the United States had such a vast uninhabited area. I suspected with good reason that the inhospitable terrain was the answer.

The blog had lots of loosely related postings about local community issues, but there were some statements about land rights. *We have a common theme here about the politics concerning 'stolen land.'*

I made more notes in Kurt's dossier. What grabbed my attention was the photo posted on the blog page. Those wide-set black eyes, thick eyebrows, stumpy nose, and those 1970s-style aviator eyeglasses were unmistakable. Definitely him. However, his eyes were puffy, suggesting he was drinkinh a lot. Yvette was right; he wasn't well.

I placed the cursor over the photo and right-clicked to save it into a new folder. I then opened it using a piece of software that allowed me to enhance different aspects of the picture. The background was what I wanted to examine. That was most telling because it set the context for where it was taken. For photos snapped of people at social gatherings, though, the photographer wasn't interested in the background, only the people. They were blind to what was behind them. It was this oversight that can produce valuable leads.

The photo appeared to have been taken on the side of a dirt road with a few Aboriginal men standing around talking. One was on horseback. There was a Nissan Exterra off to the side, but its license plate could barely be seen in the frame.

I zoomed in. South Australia was printed in small letters across the bottom and listed seven characters. The letter 'S' then three numbers followed by three letters. A firm lead. With this data I could find out whom he was with and where they were.

I typed the words *South Australia* and the number plate into the search engine and hit the enter key.

"Arkaroola" appeared. Now I *was* intrigued. Then I realized I'd be late for work, so I phoned Stoner.

He exploded, yelling, "You're supposed to be photographing the sidewalk for that law firm. The lawyer and the plaintiff are waiting!"

I glanced at my watch to discover that my 'quick search' took well over an hour; I was late, and I still hadn't had my croissant.

"Hey, I had some personal matters to sort out. I'll be there as soon as I can. Let them know."

"You might be taking more time off than you think."
"What's that mean?"

"You heard me. Do you need me to spell it out?" I cracked my knuckles. "Fuck you, Stoner."

"What!"

I could imagine his eyes protruding. "You heard me. Do you need *me* to spell it out? F U—"

"You've overstepped the mark."

"Not yet I haven't. *This* oversteps the mark," and I let him have it. "If you were any more stupid, you'd have to be watered twice a week along with the office plants. I quit! Stick the job in the crack of your ass and photograph *that* for the lawyers."

I cut the call.

Six

I phoned Yvette Kerslake and said, "I found him. Well, sort of. I know where he was recently, anyway."

"You have!" she began to stutter. "That's wonderful news. Where? What's he doing? Please bring him home. Today! Now!"

Her words flew at me like a shower of meteors in a science fiction movie. "Steady. It's a progress report to see what you want to do."

"You need to go and get him." Her tone was sharp.

"Well that's going to be a problem," I said, and I sucked a breath into my lungs. I knew this wasn't going to be a simple discussion. "First, I have no authority to bring anyone back from anywhere—that's called kidnapping. Second, I think he's in Australia, and the last time I looked at a map, it was a big place, a long way from here. Third, you haven't hired me yet. And with this case I'll need more than the usual one-week retainer."

The line went silent. *Was it the retainer?* She offered one week in advance when we met, so I couldn't imagine that asking for two weeks' pay would be a problem. She appeared to have plenty. *Maybe I should have done a credit check?*

Her voice came back on the line. "Australia? What's he doing?" Her tone was more controlled.

Okay, it wasn't the money. "Not sure, but it seems to me that he's meeting with some Australian Aborigines. The words 'land rights' mean anything to you?"

"We need to talk."

"Yep, that's what we are doing right now."

"No, you need to come here so we can talk." Her voice was becoming shrill, bordering on what sounded like distress.

There was little chance of her phone being bugged, or people watching her, so I wasn't sure why I needed another drive to Boston. Still, she was a person who needed to be in control, and this was too emotional a discovery to try to discuss rationally over the phone. Anyway, I thought it would be good to collect my retainer now that I had quit my job. The notion that I still needed to pay the upcoming winter's heating bill hadn't occurred to me when I blew up at Stoner.

"Sure, I'll be there by noon. Cash is king, so stop at the bank, and—"

"Yes, I know, I'll have a black coffee ready. I have cash. Come."

* * *

"How do you know he's in Australia?" she asked, her tone short.

I opened my briefcase and took out the dossier I started to compile. In it was the photo I printed from the Internet. I had circled the enlargement of the Nissan's license plate number.

She looked at it and studied the people before she read the plate number. "South Australia. How soon can you go?"

"Whoa. Let's take a step back. Why would he be in Australia? Who are these people? He obviously knows them. See the way they're standing around talking. They appear to be friends."

"I don't know, but I suspect he is involved in some business venture."

"What are you talking about? Business? Do you mean he's selling artwork? Giving art lessons? You didn't mention any business ventures before." I lowered my voice and leaned forward, "You need to tell me the truth. What's happening? What's with the syringes?"

"He has a drinking problem." She swallowed then continued, "When some people drink, they get happy. When others drink, they want to fight—"

"I know," I said, "the remaining drunks breakdown and cry."

"I wish it was that simple. When Kurt drinks, and it's often, he talks politics. He gets serious, worked up, agitated. He contests the notion of class egalitarianism. His discussions can become quite undignified. I'm afraid that after years of drinking, his ability to reason has been weakened. Combine that with his artist's intense imagination, his longing for nostalgic tribal ways, and—" She stared at her hands.

"Okay, now we're getting somewhere. Australian Aborigines have a long-standing petition with their government for recognition in their constitution for the land they say was never ceded to colonial settlers. You think he is involved in some sort of political activism with these people?"

"He was fixated about land rights. Being free of government meddling." She shook her head. "I never thought he'd do anything like this." "So, I take it that was a 'yes'? He's talked about Australia?"

She glanced back at me. "Over the years, he's been invited to speak to indigenous peoples in Canada and Central America. So, him talking to Australian Aborigines about this type of thing doesn't come as a surprise. He raised the possibility over a year ago, but I never thought anything would come of it."

"Fine, let's work with the hypothesis that he's in Australia meeting with Aboriginals who are involved in the land rights movement. Why would he leave and not tell you? Why simply disappear?"

"He's done this before because he knows I'd stop him. Each time I had an idea where he might be, and I brought him home. Mostly Canada. Those absences were easy to explain. Now he's on the verge of ruining his reputation. He could jeopardize his standing by getting involved in these issues. They are not mainstream politics he's preaching, they're—"

I thought about the blog post and finished her sentence, "—they're on the lunatic fringe. Come on, who believes there's a lost world where indigenous people can live free?" I resisted adding, 'Without the IRS knowing.'

She glared at me. My words had found their mark. She snapped back, fire in her voice, "Are you referring to the crimes committed against American Indians, driven from their land, sacred pray sites desecrated, hunted almost to extinction? White invasion resulted in obliteration."

I steadied myself. I knew I was in for a verbal broadside.

"He has wounds. Wounds of the heart. He lives in a wilderness of emotional pain. That's the reason for the syringes. Traditionally, some American Indians used mescaline for rituals. Now, people use it to see ordinary things differently, to find beauty where it was overlooked, or ugliness no one thought existed. Others used it to allow their minds to drift, to be creative. Kurt read that it could be used to treat alcoholism. He couldn't get it, so he used some other kind of hallucinogenic."

I let her tidal wave of emotion wash over me. She seemed to need to project the illusion of a quaint, pleasant life. It was in keeping with the image of an art gallery curator. She needed to fashion a life of tranquil comfort while entertaining her non-mainstream political thoughts.

Nevertheless, the lecture on the mescaline rituals sounded crazy to a practical guy.

I scanned the room. The signs were there—the furniture, the soft furnishings, the artwork on the walls, the photographs on the fireplace mantel, the way she dressed, and her manner. It

38

all made sense. Kurt was the vehicle for this lifestyle. He offered her the ways and means to achieve what she desired while dabbling in leftist politics.

So, I was right; it wasn't his looks.

She wanted—needed—to bring him home to save public face. More precisely, to save herself from being disgraced. Either way, she wanted me to retrieve him. I suspected any PI agency she approached would have turned down her request. Perhaps they had, and that's why she contacted me through her gallery friend.

What do I say?

I had the retainer in my wallet. I could tell her 'yes,' have a trip to Australia, see a few iconic sights, have my picture taken with a koala, come back and tell her I wasn't successful, but that wasn't the person I was. Or, I could charge her for the work I've done, and hand back the rest; wish her all the best.

I met her square on, ready to give her money back when her green eyes met mine. I stopped. Her short chestnut-colored bangs accentuated a desperate portrait in them. Women can be vulnerable. Even this one. Body armor can't stop all bullets, and this woman's emotional armor resembled a colander.

I buckled under the pressure. "Sure, I'll go, and see what I can do. However, I'll be honest; it'll be expensive, and there's no guarantee of success."

"Money's not a problem."

She stood and walked me to the door, asking as she went, "You do have a passport?"

"Yep." I had traveled to Scotland with Ellen several times.

"Good, email me the details. I'll make the flight reservations and get the visa you'll need online. I assume you'll want to fly Qantas, a superb airline. It's the one I use when I travel the Pacific." She paused. "You'll need to work out where to go once you are in-country and where you'll stay."

"The capital of South Australia is Adelaide, so I need to fly there. I'll conduct some more background investigations before I go, to see if I can get a better fix on where he is exactly. South Australia is twice the size of Texas, so there'll be a lot of real estate to wander around if I don't narrow it down. I need to work out where this place, Arkaroola, is in relation to Adelaide, and how to get there."

"That retainer isn't going to go far, so let me increase it. I'll do an electronic transfer today."

Money sure isn't an issue. Made a change from working for insurance companies. I needed a crowbar to separate them from the money they owed me.

I cleared my throat. "We need to talk about the realities of bringing him home."

Her eyes engaged mine the way a defiant child would stare at a parent. "I'll take you through the situation and highlight the problems. There's a bucket load of them," I said.

I drew in a deep breath. "*If* I find him, I can't arrest him. He hasn't done anything wrong in relation to the law. If I were to somehow detain him, I'd be up for a charge of kidnapping, false imprisonment, or whatever the Australian authorities have in their statute books. Whatever laws they have could mean me going to jail, so that's out. Even if I were Matt Damon, I'd have the problem of how to transport him secretly to the airport. Picture it. I'd be escorting a handcuffed and blindfolded man, no doubt with duct tape over his mouth, through the Immigration and Customs control points. Australia is an island continent a long, long way from Massachusetts. If I find him, he'll have to *want* to come home. Otherwise, it's a waste of your money and my time."

I halted to let that register. "You still want me to do it?"

She seemed to be forcing herself to stand still. "I'll electronically transfer the funds this afternoon, then email you your e-ticket details."

As I walked to my jeep, my thoughts should have been on generating a plan to find Kurt Kerslake, but they were drifting back to Rose and Drew.

Taking on this case meant the man in the black BMW would be a step ahead. He was a smooth-talker, and I didn't need Sophie to point out the clock was ticking.

Seven

After landing at New York's JFK Airport on Tuesday morning, I made my way through the terminal to the departure gate. I was looking for Qantas flight QF108, destination Sydney, Australia. The flight had one stop in Los Angeles.

Having cleared security and immigration, I arrived at the gate on time. My flight to New York started at Bradley International Airport, which was the closet airport to East Longmeadow. It was situated mid-way between Hartford, Connecticut, and Springfield, Massachusetts, yet closer than Boston's Logan Airport.

While I was in the departure lounge at Bradley, Sophie texted me. She said that Rose and Drew were off to Europe. It must have come up at the cinema last night because when Sophie went to the delicatessen for her morning coffee, Rose told her. Sophie said she hid her shock and feigned joy but texted me as soon as she could get away from the scrum of cooing women milled around Rose. I appreciated Sophie leaving off what could have been a post-script, 'I told you so.'

If today was a fish, I think I would've thrown it back. However, I knew the risks of taking on this case. Standing in the boarding line gave me time to reflect. I wasn't devastated. I wasn't jealous, envious, or hurt. It certainly wasn't deep affection I had for Rose. Perhaps it was what I recalled love to be. Somewhere inside those thoughts, I knew she wasn't for me; otherwise, I wouldn't be standing in line.

With shuffling footsteps, I inched forward in the queue for economy passengers. The line was long, so I resigned myself to a bit of a wait.

I flipped through the pages of my passport and saw the visa stamps for the United Kingdom. The last one was six years ago when Ellen and I last visited her family in Scotland. That was the year before she passed away. I was reminiscing about our trip when my eye caught the figure of a woman in the adjacent business class line. *Yvette?*

The woman showed the Qantas steward her boarding pass and passport and moved through to the aerobridge. My legs had the sensation of being trapped in swamp mud. I wanted to race and catch her but couldn't move. Knowing what airport security was like, if I did, I'd be hauled into the security office.

So, I waited. I'd see her after boarding and find out what the hell she was doing. *She must be hemorrhaging money if she can drop everything and fly business class to Australia.*

Minutes later, I made my way to my seat on the Boeing 747 and placed my netbook computer in the overhead locker. While I was sorting out my backpack, I sensed someone standing next to me, so I moved out of the way. Instead, I heard Yvette's voice.

"I was going to tell you, but you must have had your cell phone switched off. Anyway, I'm coming with you. You won't have to kidnap him. I'll convince him he needs to come home."

"Shh, Yvette! Some words should never be uttered on an aircraft, *kidnap* is one. Please be subtle."

"I'm sitting upfront. I'll see you when we land in Sydney. We'll talk while we wait for our connecting flight to Adelaide."

"Business class? Convenient. Was that so I can't go forward and tell you my thoughts on having you tag along?"

She didn't answer then strolled up the narrow aisle. I had to save my lecture for when we arrived.

As I rummaged through my backpack for an old copy of an E. Howard Hunt spy thriller, I heard the words, "G'day mate," coming from a deep, sultry voice. She had an accent I hadn't heard often. I saw a woman in a pink western-style shirt, matching pink cowgirl hat, and black denim jeans. She was older than I was, perhaps by five years.

In a bubbly voice that reminded me of Dolly Parton, she asked, "You going to sit down or what?"

"Sorry." Despite my six-foot frame, I tried to melt into the seat for the twenty-three-hour flight Down Under.

"No worries, mate, I'm keen to get moving. I've been away for three months and want to get home. Know what I mean?" She flung her carry-on bag and hat into the vacant space in the overhead locker and slammed it closed.

A no-nonsense woman.

We were the only two sitting in our row of three on the starboard side. She sat on the aisle, and I was in the middle. After we were airborne and the seatbelt sign was off, I indicated to her that I'd move to the window seat so she could have more room. I was about to settle into the tempo of waiting out the back-to-back trans-continental/trans-Pacific flights, when she said, "Name's Faye Bellcroft," and stuck out her hand. She had a sturdy grip. I was impressed. Most people want to put on a set of noise-cancelling headphones, but I got the impression she had no interest in the in-flight entertainment system.

I introduced myself. She told me she was an entertainer who had landed a contract to sing Australian folk songs on a cruise liner sailing the Mediterranean. It had stopped in ports across North Africa. She was flying home via New York because she wanted to buy a special guitar brand there. The name didn't mean anything to me. I pretended to understand as she described the guitar's strings and fret spacing's.

"I was excited. This was a big gig for me. Not many Australian women get that kind of chance, but once we were out to sea, I realized I couldn't swim. See, I come from a place that only has ten inches of rain a year. The ground is so dry when it does rain, the place floods." She laughed. "Forget about seasickness. That's nothing if you're afraid of drowning. It took me a week to muster the courage to go on deck. I was so scared of what would happen if I fell overboard."

I nodded knowingly, but having grown up with ponds, lakes, and rivers, I could swim well and never feared water.

"You heard about that cruise ship the *Costa Concordia* that ran aground on rocks off the coast of Italy? That would have been my worst nightmare," she said.

I sensed this was a real issue for her, and she was glad to be going home. *That would have been horrible; three months on a swaying ship knowing you couldn't swim to save yourself.*

"I don't know much about cruises, only what I've read in travel brochures."

"Can you swim?"

"Yeah, sure can. I'm a certified scuba diver."

"Cruises used to be a place for the newlywed, overfed, and almost dead, and it hasn't changed. It's like a nursing home that sails." She started to fidget in her seat. "I subscribe to Dorothy's philosophy 'there's no place like home'," and cast her unfocused gaze out the window.

* * *

As the minutes turned into hours, and many hours passed, the dull boredom of the long-haul flight set in. I could see what Faye meant about there being no place like home. Seems exciting on travel websites, but they never tell you about the flying. Nevertheless, I wasn't doing this for relaxation. It was work. I wondered what kind of man Kurt would prove to be when I tracked him down.

Faye and I talked on and off during the flight about lots of things, from horoscope signs to whether there was a God, but mainly about Faye's work and her new life when she got home.

She said she had a light-bulb moment and wanted to complete her high school equivalency and study education at university. She wanted to vent. It was strange because as I listened, I grew attracted to this determined woman. Her face was covered with freckles, stretching from cheek to cheek the way a constellation of stars spreads across the night sky. There was sincerity in her words and the way she presented. I got the impression she played no emotional games.

Later, after we were served dinner, Yvette appeared at the end of the row. "Comfortable?"

I wanted to tell her what I thought of her travel arrangements, but having that approach not work well with Stoner, I reconsidered and decided to save it until I submitted my final invoice. "Sure, no complaints."

"Okay. I wanted to check on you before I go to sleep. I'll have the steward bring you your usual." She smiled and cast a catty glance at Faye, then she was gone.

I wasn't comfortable with the exchange, and I could tell Faye was less than impressed with the glare she received. She was no doubt trying to work out our relationship, especially after Yvette's 'bring you your usual' remark. I suspected that Faye realized Yvette wasn't someone I'd met in the departure lounge to compare travel tips.

"So, what are you doing in Australia?" By the way she said it, she might as well have added, *with her*.

"I'm in real estate. I'm helping her find some property. She's my client." It was partly true. I was helping her find 'some property,' which happened to be her husband. The real estate slant was what PIs call a *pretext*. It's a polite way of saying I'm lying. But, in my case, I wanted to think I was demonstrating *discretion*.

"Hmm, bet she spends her days obsessing about what nail polish she'll wear." Faye turned up her mouth. "I'd say she was a fifty-pairs-of-shoes girl, but you don't seem to be that kind of guy."

I shrugged. "She pays my invoice."

I could see Faye didn't warm to her. She seemed to me to be a good judge of character, and I added that to the list of her impressive qualities. After Yvette's display of bad manners, any thought that this trip was going to be enjoyable was jettisoned along the aircraft's vapor trail. I wanted to reunite Yvette with Kurt and get back home...like Dorothy. However, this woman sitting beside me had a magnetic pull.

Minutes later a flight attendant appeared with a large tumbler containing a generous amount of Scotch whiskey. Next to it was a small bowl of ice cubes. He winked. "Someone special sent this back for you. Would you like ice?"

"No thanks, I'll have it as it is." As I reached for the glass, I knew the awkwardness this was going to present for Faye, and anyway, it's lonely drinking without a partner. So, I added, "Oh, she was going to order two drinks, one for my traveling companion here." I indicated Faye with a polite tilt of my head.

The steward, who must have thought I was in some romantic relationship with Yvette, seemed dumbstruck. Trying to keep his composure, he forced a smile. "Of course, sir, my oversight. I'll bring that straight away. Whiskey, ma'am?"

"Rum. Cuban if you've got it. Neat, no ice," came her words without hesitation. She reached across the vacant seat between us and squeezed my arm. "You Yanks went without Cuban rum for decades. You slapped that trade embargo on those Communists devils back in the 60s because they wanted to incinerate your country with Russian nuclear missiles. You don't know what you've missed for all those years."

We drank and had another. I tried her rum, and she was right. Unlike Scotch—complex and alluring—this was smooth, potent, and euphoric. We talked until the cabin lights were switched off. As I drifted to sleep, my thoughts were of her touch. I recalled the caress of Rose's hand when I picked up Sophie. I wanted to believe Faye's wasn't friendship, but *affection*. Regardless, with my recent run of bad luck, it was probably some dreamy illusion that my alcohol-fueled mind had generated, like one of those romantic painters' landscapes.

As I gave in to the urge to sleep, I was awash with the desire to hold her, to run my hands over her skin and imagined her arms around me. In those moments before sleep took hold, my thoughts stirred a yearning in me. Faye triggered something in me more profound than anything I had for Rose. This was more than a memory of love. It was the difference between being in love and loving someone.

* * *

The crew switched on the cabin lights. But I was already awake. Their movement moments earlier disturbed me. I don't sleep well at the best of times, but on an aircraft, less so. And having a few strong drinks probably didn't help.

Faye moved, adjusted the thin blanket she was wrapped in and looked around. Her gaze finally settled on me.

I smiled. "Good morning. Hope you slept well. Coffee?"

She took the edge of the blanket and rubbed her eyes. She was without pretense as if we had known each other for a long time. She didn't have a young face, but at that hour of the morning, her features were tender.

Her expression suddenly exploded into a bright smile. "You're the first bloke I've slept with that's been decent to me in the morning. Usually, they're hungover, bad-tempered, and smelling like—" Her gaze searched my face. "You know. I've never had a bloke offer *me* coffee."

Slept with her? I gave her a bashful grin. I suppose I did, even if it was a stretch of the truth. I wondered where this was going, so I indulged her. I must admit, after last night's thoughts, the picture she painted of us together was provocative.

The Qantas steward appeared at the end of our row holding a small tray in one hand and a pot in the other. "Coffee?"

She reached for my arm, grabbed my hand, and said, "You meant it." She laughed then returned her attention to the steward. "No dear, I take tea, but thanks."

He poured me a long black and moved on. As I sipped the rich, bitter liquid, my heart raced with the thought she'd sown. The sensation of Faye's hand on mine sent a tingle of magic through me.

"You staying in Australia long? I could use a bloke like you in my life," she murmured. "Can you fix things, or do you work in a real estate office?"

To my surprise, I heard myself say, "I'm a Renaissance man," but before I could explain, a flight attendant materialized with the breakfast trays and all the commotion that accompanied serving, so the discussion was lost. There was no doubt I was finding Faye Bellcroft captivating. There's nothing more beautiful than discovering an honest person.

* * *

When the aircraft came to a halt at the Sydney terminal, passengers were busy getting ready to disembark. Bags were being pulled from the overhead lockers, and the aisles filled with travelers.

I asked, "Where do you live?"

She stopped what she was doing and faced me. "You asking to see me again? Hey, I live in 'the bush.' Someplace you've never heard of, or ever will."

"The bush?"

"Yep, where I come from is back-of-beyond. A place where two cars arriving at an intersection at the same time is considered a traffic jam." She stared at me, "You're an attentive, thoughtful listener. I had a good time talking to you, but where I live—it wouldn't be your comfort zone. Anyway, you're wearing a wedding ring. I never get involved with married men." She motioned with her head toward the business class cabin. "She's lucky. Really lucky. Too bad we didn't meet before you two did. I'm in need of a good bloke."

I'd worn my wedding ring for so long I never gave it any thought. *How dumb am I?* This meeting new women stuff wasn't coming naturally. "Yeah, I'm wearing a ring, but—"

She shrugged. "She's not your sister. So, who is she?"

"I told you, she's my client." Like Pinocchio, I could feel my nose growing. I wasn't sounding convincing, not even to myself.

"Client? What sort of client?"

"I'm helping her find some property."

"Oh sure, and I believe in the Tooth Fairy. I work in the entertainment industry. I hear all sorts of stories from all kinds of people, and I can tell you yours doesn't stack-up. Anyway, I'm not going to push it, but I'll let you in on a secret. Whatever it is you're doing, that wedding ring suggests you're trying to have a bit of fun on the side." She flashed a cynical sneer.

We were moving with the crush of people exiting the aircraft. I had to talk fast. "I'm not married. I was. I'm a widower. My wife died five years ago. I miss her a lot, that's

50

why I still wear the ring. I'm a bit rusty at this type of thing. I'm not used to—"

Before I could finish, she said, "Darling, I can see you're a soft-hearted bloke, but I need a practical guy around my house because I'm going back to study. I want someone I can talk to, but more importantly, someone I can believe in, not someone who'll play with my mind."

Her face filled with compassion, but like the clouds drifting overhead, she disappeared across the aerobridge and into the crowded terminal. She was gone.

Eight

I could see Yvette ahead of me in the custom's line. Being in business class, she exited first, moving rapidly through the queue. Being an economy passenger, I was in a holding pattern. Once inside the terminal, I found Yvette waiting.

She gave me a curt nod. "I want to do some shopping, so let's meet at the Qantas Lounge. I'm allowed to admit a guest. We can talk there."

I needed some time to think about what had happened with Faye. I was still trying to reconcile my anger about Drew's *tour de force*, but Faye's rebuff left me with a wound I feared would leave a scar.

What would Sophie have advised? Perhaps talking about it with her on Skype would help. I was out of my depth with this dating stuff, and as much as I wanted to get to the bottom of what Yvette was doing here, I didn't want to have an argument about her stowing away. "Sure, I'll have a look around too," I said.

We walked along the concourse in different directions. Her stride took her to some brand-name fashion boutique.

As I listened to flight boarding announcements over the PA system, I decided I needed to think like a chess player and come up with an offense to neutralize Yvette's check. I'd walked only a few paces when it came to me. After thinking it through a couple of times, I was happy with my plan, but I'd need to wait. As in a chess game, timing is everything.

* * *

Although airport shops aren't indicative of the country, they do reflect life in the wider community, so Sydney Airport was interesting in that regard. I took an instant liking to the way Australians moved and interacted. They were friendlier than

52

Americans, more apt to greet you with a smile or a 'G'day,' and people called me *mate* even though we'd never met before. I liked the country. People were in less of a hurry than the States. The Australian accent was much different from the English accents I was used to when I traveled to the United Kingdom with Ellen. And different from Ellen's Scottish inflection. From my brief encounter with the people I overheard, I realized that Australians had unique idioms, so when I saw an Australian slang dictionary in the concourse book shop, I bought it.

There were a few other books I saw on travel destinations within Australia, and one on the Flinders Ranges in South Australia. An expensive large picture book with historical facts and commentary, including Arkaroola. I thumbed through it, snapping photos of noteworthy pages using my smartphone's camera. A tactic that was less conspicuous than writing notes and faster and cheaper than paying the price asked. I was conscious that if the salespeople saw me, they might make a point of telling me they weren't in business to be my personal library.

During the Cold War days of the spy-game, operatives used miniature cameras to secretly photograph documents using roll film. Now, with a cell phone with a two-fifty-six gigabyte micro-SD card, a person could steal a truckload of information, never having to reload film.

There was a book on Australian wildlife I thought worthy of a quick look. When I browsed the pages at the end that discussed the venomous critters, I flinched. Amongst the varieties of spiders and biting and stinging insects, there were snakes! I hated snakes and couldn't even hold the book knowing there were photos of them. An irrational fear, but fear all the same. I then could relate to Faye's fear of drowning. In all my years of living in Massachusetts, I only saw one snake, and that was a garter snake. Garters have never been known to kill a human because their venom was so mild and their mouths not well suited to biting big animals, such as people. But, it's the way they move and their expressionless faces that make them appear so evil.

I closed the book and went to wait at the entrance to the Qantas Lounge. Yvette appeared with a bag stenciled with R.M. Williams and waved me in. When we were in the lounge, she showed me her purchase. Originally, R.M. Williams was a saddler and maker of stockmen's accessories, now his company catered to trendy urbanites. In her bag was a pair of boots.

"What's this about?" I asked as I couldn't help thinking she was trying to imitate Faye in some jealous way.

"I need to blend in. Isn't that what PIs do? Blend in?"

I recalled Faye's throwaway line about her footwear collection. Did this pair make fifty-one, two, or three? There was no doubt that Yvette had an eye for fashion. Her tall, angular features were stunning. However, her attitude was a concern. I suspected it was a tactic to avoid discussing why she came.

Time to spring my trap. "So, you were going to explain being here?" I said, interrupting her fashion show.

She reached for her glass of Sauvignon Blanc and rested back in the armchair. "You said it yourself. Kurt won't come back unless he's in handcuffs, so I'm here to persuade him."

"What makes you think he'll listen to you?"

She leaned toward me, her hands on her knees. "I persuaded *you* to find him."

"Touché, but you didn't hire me to be your bodyguard. Close personal protection isn't a service I offer. I go alone from here. Book yourself into a hotel and see what's on at the Opera House. We'll meet-up after I find him." *Checkmate.*

Nonetheless, she wasn't paying attention. She began tapping and scrolling on her computer tablet. Then she turned the screen toward me. "Is that enough to change your mind?"

She had the transfer screen for her bank account displayed. There was a sum listed, and under it was my account number at the credit union in East Longmeadow. I thought I had her ensnared, but she was about to block my check. That was a lot of money.

"It'll certainly buy a new set of snow tires for the jeep."

She offered me a bemused smile. "I'm starting to get used to your dry sense of humor."

I didn't consider this scenario in my planning. She watched me consider the new terms and conditions. I couldn't disguise the fact I was wavering on accepting.

She raised her eyebrows. "Do I transfer the cash, or book myself into some harbor-side accommodation?"

Hell! I was supposed to be the one doing the ambushing.

Her finger hovered over the transfer button. "Well? Do we have a deal or not?"

Nine

T he connecting flight to Adelaide was announced. I lifted my glass and threw back the Cuban rum. "Okay, but I run the operation. You're coming along to convince Kurt in case he throws a tantrum."

Again, she wasn't listening. She gathered up her shopping. I could only be angry with myself since I had succumbed. I held my glass up to the light and watched the film of the remaining liquid slowly recede down the sides. Faye was right. Cuban rum was the smoothest liquor I'd ever had. I could easily develop a taste for it.

* * *

After we landed and once in the taxi, I instructed the driver to take us to the Hilton Hotel on Adelaide's Victoria Square. Located in the center of the city, the hotel was well situated for me to organize for our expedition to the outback. Although I had seen Sydney Airport, this was my first encounter with the Australian countryside. I scanned the houses and streets as the taxi wove its way through the traffic east in to the city center. Reminiscent of southern California there were single-story buildings and neat streetscapes with eucalyptus trees. The weather was mild compared to New England, and the buildings reflected this in their construction that didn't include all the provisions for snowstorms. A pleasing sight.

My eyes were getting heavy, and my head bumped the taxi's side window when I momentarily nodded off. I was exhausted and wanted to sleep.

A few minutes later, we arrived at our hotel. At the reception counter, I fought to keep my eyes open while Yvette asked if they had a city view room with a king-size bed on one of the upper floors. I only wanted a room, but because she was paying, I thought I'd test her goodwill. I leaned on the counter, and said, "Same for me." Without a moment's hesitation, she swiped her credit card through the e-terminal and entered her PIN.

At the door to my room, I bade her good night. Suppressing a yawn, I said, "See you in the morning. We can discuss our plans at breakfast. Does 7 a.m. suit?"

"What? It's only four in the afternoon. You're going to sleep now?" "I've had it. Need my beauty rest. Seven okay?"

"Sure, but you'll miss out on the fun tonight."

"I'm off duty. No close personal protection tonight. If you go out, you're on your own."

"After what I paid you, I'd expect your services all day, every day."

I inserted the plastic swipe card into the locking mechanism and heard the bolt retract. As I pushed the door open, I glanced left at her doing the same. It was difficult to focus, but I could make out Yvette standing there in her black leather skirt. I wondered what Kurt was thinking when he left her. I was sure the waters of his mind were dark and shadowy. How could he not see what he had in her? What would I'd think when I met him? And, I *was* going to meet him. I was determined to find out what this was about. What kind of man walks out on a life like that?

I didn't have the energy to study the photographic notes I made earlier, but I was resolute to stay awake long enough to send Sophie an email asking her to run a few background checks for me.

Ten

I was surprised to see she was at breakfast before me. Yvette was in her gym attire, obviously having finished a workout. I could never bring myself to go to a gym with the full-length mirrors, rows of machines, funky music, and mineral water in colors that matched whatever Lycra you were wearing. Always thought they were places one went to be seen rather than to get in shape.

Guests were moving to-and-fro, and a few milled around the buffet. She sat at a table off to the side with her back against the wall, giving the table visual command of the room. Made me grin. The last thing a PI wants was to be noticed, and she was true to her word and trying to blend in.

I had a plan for the expedition, so when we finished exchanging niceties, I briefed her. "I'll rent a vehicle and meet you back here then we head north."

After breakfast, Yvette wandered off to pack, while I phoned places to rent a four-wheel drive. They all had reasonable rates, but one offered to drop it off within the hour, so I went with them.

As I completed the paperwork and loaded my duffle into the Holden, I thought about Faye. On occasion, you meet someone and wonder if life would be good with them. When you're in a relationship, you have a built-in moral shield that forces you *not* to wonder, because it wouldn't be right. When you're single, and you meet people, you view them with a different eye. I viewed Faye that way. Although she'd made it clear she wasn't interested, saying, 'I need a practical guy who can fix things...' Even though she was hard to put out of my mind, I probably needed to resign myself to the fact it would always be an unsatisfied itch. *Perhaps if I thought about her as one of those infatuations one has while on vacation, the ache would go.*

My smartphone vibrated. Sophie's email had arrived with the details I'd requested.

* * *

I eased the Holden into the morning traffic, shifting the gears as we left the last set of traffic lights on the main arterial road out of Adelaide. We were heading north to a place called Copley; five kilometers north of Leigh Creek, about eight hours' drive.

A simple route. I needed to drive north to a place called Port Augusta. From there, it was slightly east, then north again to our destination.

Although it was late October, and New England was entering the autumn equinox, it was spring in Australia. It felt as if I was being given a second chance at something, still air, green countryside, clear blue skies, and warmth. As we traveled along the Princes Highway toward Port Augusta, I glanced at everything: the vehicles on the roads, the buildings, and the landscape. Manifestly different from driving along the Mass Pike, there was flat countryside with wheat and other cereal crops growing on immense acreages. No forests common in New England. The only trees were *gums*—eucalypts—and other native species. I had seen them in the glossy picture books at Sydney Airport, but couldn't recall their names. They grew in small stands here and there off the side of the highway, or in the distance around homesteads.

I placed the Holden in cruise control and steadied myself for the journey by suggesting to Yvette that we listen to some music. She busied herself with the vehicle's FM radio, tuning this station and then that until she located some classical melodies. Once we passed Port Wakefield, the reception faded, and we lost the music to atmospheric static. That was a relief because I wasn't a fan of classical music.

There were a few AM stations, but Yvette discounted them and opted for what she had on her smartphone. She had an eclectic collection. Having listened to the aria by Verdi about unrequited love, I kept one eye on the road as I scrolled through her collection. I left a few hippy rock operas behind and switched to an old Peter Sarstedt's song, *Where do you Go to (My Lovely)*. The open vastness of the landscape gave the impression that the vehicle's speed was slow. The hum of the engine made me drift into a trance, but I came back when I heard, '...shake off their lowly born tags...'. How wrong I was about Kurt providing the income for her lifestyle.

Sophie's email had briefed me on the background and credit checks she ran. Yvette was 'old money' *...an only child of parents, who owned a house in Boston's Beacon Hill neighborhood, one of the most expensive neighborhoods in Boston. Her father is a partner in a law firm that has offices in Boston, New York, and Washington. The firm's clients were banks and investment houses until the financial crisis of 2008 when it did an almost overnight shift in its specialty to IP— intellectual property. The firm now represents many software giants.*

Sophie's briefing said that Yvette was wealthy in her own right and didn't need Kurt's income. In fact, a credit check showed that although his sales generated a generous salary that faded in comparison to Yvette's investments.

She had graduated with a BA in art history from Smith College, majoring in art and artefacts of American Indians. She went on to take her master's in art installations—displays and displaying artworks—from Harvard. If that wasn't enough, she's a member of the Daughters of the American Revolution.

With that sort of background, no wonder she was appointed curator of the American Indian Collection.

Sarstedt's words, 'They say that when you get married it'll be to a millionaire,' couldn't be further from the truth. I wondered why she married him. *What was it that she saw in him? Why didn't he see the opportunity he had in her and her unblinking commitment to him?*

Yvette reached across the dash and changed the song to something upbeat.

Seemed a good opportunity to raise the issue. "So, what have you been reading?" I said, trying to get inside her head.

As an investigator, I found a person's bookshelf as telling as any other question. If people didn't have books in their house, that told a story. If they did and there were only a few, that too told a story. When I read the titles, they revealed some insights into their mind.

"Art history mostly." She slanted her head to regard me with suspicion.

I maneuvered the conversation to reveal more. "I thought you'd be the type to read books such as *The Greening of America*, or *Atlas Shrugged*. That kind of thing."

"I've read those in my youth. I'm interested in clever people's visions and thinking about how the world they hoped for might come about."

I regarded lefties with some reservation because I thought they spent a lot of time thinking about the world, but not doing much about it. "Does Kurt read much?"

"What are you getting at?"

I could sense her bristle as if there was static electricity in the air. "How did he come up with those ideas? They're not grounded. Is this some publicity stunt to drive up his sales? I'll be honest with you, I ran a credit check."

61

I was sure there were flashes of high voltage sparking inside her head as she spoke.

"My trust takes care of me financially, so I can concentrate on the promotion of art and my patronage of the fine arts. I take care of Kurt, so he can paint. Unfortunately, discrimination influenced his identity in a big way. His art was a way of coping with it, and exposing it, but he succumbed to drink. After a while *it* consumed *him*. Our relationship slowly sank into days where he had long sulking moods. He became depressed. It wasn't pleasant. Depression isn't kind. I worked hard to shield him from the public backlash of his drinking, but in recent times, his drinking got out of hand."

"And now he's taking hallucinogenic drugs. Is that the source of his strange ideas?"

Yvette turned away. She spoke to me but stared out at the countryside. "I wanted a child. We tried. He couldn't deliver." She bowed her head. "Depression has left him incapable of—"

I flinched. "Sorry."

"For what? These things happen."

I wasn't game to tell her my joke about how I felt better once I gave up on hope, so I said, "We still need to find a way through the darkness."

She didn't comment. Just stared out the window.

As the countryside sped past at 110 kilometers an hour, I reassured her, "I'll find him."

Eleven

At a small town called Crystal Brook we stopped at a petrol station for fuel. An interesting town, the sign said it was named after a natural spring that fed the nearby creek. Perhaps it was given the name *Brook* instead of *Creek* by some nostalgic English pioneer.

"Goin' to be a big rain," came the voice of a mechanic who passed us on his way to the garage. His overalls were embroidered with a logo and name of some farm maintenance business. A young man, probably in his late-twenties, but with the appearance that he'd worked for thirty years. He had creases in his face the sun had etched-in that had accumulated with grease.

I smiled. "Looks clear to me," and glanced at the sky.

He pointed northwest. "For now, but you see those clouds, they're goin' to bring a drenchin. Where you headed?"

"Five kilometers north of Leigh Creek. Copley."

"Isn't likely you'll make it. Radio news is saying that roads to the north are goin' to be washed out. Which way are you thinking' of goin?" "Port Augusta, then to Leigh Creek."

"If you are keen to get there, I'd be going to Laura, then I'd follow the Tarcowie Road to Orroroo. If you make it that far, then head north to Hawker. Doubt you'll get there though, that's where the worst of it will be. What are ya driving'?"

"That Holden," I said, indicating the rental next to the petrol pump, Yvette in the front passenger's seat.

"Hmm, lacks what you need to operate in the bush."

Was he talking about the vehicle or Yvette?

"I can tell you're a tourist. Canada?"

"The States. Massachusetts. Ever been there?"

63

"Nope. Furthest I've been is Melbourne. Didn't like it. Anyway, be careful crossin' creeks." With a thoughtful expression he added, "If the water comes up too high, it'll lift the vehicle. You'll float, be swept away with the rest of the debris. It's the speed of the water, the rocks, tree stumps that will to the damage. Has no mercy. You can only pray they'll find what's left of you..." He let the end of his warning hang.

I could see why he seemed older than his years. People out here obviously grew up fast. Life was sombering, unforgiving.

"Thanks, mate," I said, hoping my voice carried a ring that suggested I was less untested than I was.

"Cheers," he said and went into the mechanic's bay to work on a truck.

I returned to the vehicle and told Yvette there was a change of plans and summarized the weather forecast. I reprogrammed the GPS, and we were off.

* * *

The mechanic was right. Soon after passing through Laura, we saw the clouds move in, dark, and threatening. Rain started to hit the windshield. I had to increase the speed of the wipers as we proceeded along the narrow road. Minutes later the sky opened, and the rain became so heavy I had to slow to a crawl to see the road. What was rolling fields were now giant catchments for stormwater. Each fold in the hilly landscape channeled the rain into a series of creeks that flowed into each other until they ended up in a larger creek.

The main creek ran alongside the road and crisscrossed it at various points, but unlike where I come from, there were no bridges, only fords. The crossings were identified with water level markers that showed how high the water was in relation to the lowest part of the ford. The top of the markers said two meters. *That's six-and-a-half feet!* This was a deadly place where nature was rarely in a mood to offer bargains.

I glanced at Yvette who was silent. Her hands gripped the shoulder restraint of the seatbelt as she bent forward trying to see the road ahead. When we approached the first creek, I stopped at the top of the slope and checked the water level. Two hundred, meaning 0.2 of a meter, or about eight inches. I opened the door and leaned out to inspect the clearance of the vehicle and the center of the wheel hubs.

With a quaking voice, Yvette exclaimed, "What are you doing?"

"Checking to see if we've got the clearance to cross."

Her face was like a caricature of a cat being tortured by the sight of a bathtub, "What are you talking about!"

"If the water level is lower than the bottom of the doors, I figure the weight of the vehicle will maintain traction, so we'll be able to cross."

With a pained stare, she asked, "You're going to drive us through *that*?"

"Hey, it's only if the vehicle becomes buoyant, we'll have a problem. You can panic then."

I could see that wasn't the right thing to say. 'Trust me' would have been equally unhelpful, so I engaged the four-wheel drive hubs and eased the vehicle into the torrent, letting the idling revs take us across.

Yvette's eyes were clenched shut.

As we started to climb the other side, the sound of the water splashing under the vehicle stopped, and the rain hitting the roof was the only noise. She opened her eyes and apologized for her panic attack.

"No worries," I said in my best imitation of an Aussie accent.

She smiled. "I suppose that won't be the end of it?"

"Best I can gauge, we've another thirty or forty kilometers to Orroroo. I suspect there'll be a few more creeks."

"More?"

"Perhaps. Maybe three or four."

We were moving again, but at a slower speed because the rain had been heavy. Then, I noticed, "Hey, the rain's easing."

She looked around as if to say, 'Oh sure!'

The rain had eased, so I picked up speed hoping to get to Orroroo as soon as we could. With each creek crossing, I checked the levels and reasoned aloud so she could understand what I was doing. Seemed to give her confidence that what I was doing was safe. Most crossings were between 0.2 and 0.3 meters—eight to twelve inches. I reminded her that under the fast-flowing dark creek water was a road.

She said, "Oh yeah, I thought it would be gooey mud."

About five kilometers from Orroroo my GPS advised that we faced the last of the creeks. My confidence was peaking having had the sage advice from the man at the petrol station, so I said to Yvette, "Hey, you have a go. You tell me about the one coming up."

With her nerves settling a bit and composure returning to her voice, she said, "Okay."

A minute after we rounded the turn and started on our approach slope I realized this creek was different, as it was about three times wider. The water was rougher with a large amount of debris floating in the current. The fact we hadn't seen any vehicles coming toward us the whole way suddenly made sense. An omen.

Yvette was leaning forward again, like a lookout in an old sailing ship's crow's nest. She eyed the water level and said, "Zero point three meters," but it was the look on her face that confirmed my reservations. She must have thought this crossing was hiding something.

"Okay," I said, "we cross this one, and we'll stop at Orroroo for the night."

She gave me a hesitating nod. "Get it over with. I need a drink."

I gave the accelerator pedal a nudge and heard the engine respond. Everything was fine until we were about mid-way into the creek when the front of the vehicle suddenly dipped as if we were falling into a ravine. There was no backing up. We were at the point of no return. So, I revved the engine and immediately heard the water being hosed all over the engine. Likely it wouldn't be long before the water was sucked into the air intake. Then, the engine would stall.

Fast or slow, it didn't seem to matter how many revs I gave it. Yvette was screaming that water was coming in under the doors. As the back end of the vehicle dropped to match the front, water ran over the hood. We were on borrowed time. When that moment came, I hoped I could get her out of the vehicle. If I were a Catholic, I would have blessed myself.

She was in her now customary position, eyes clenched, grasping the shoulder strap, but this time she had her feet on the seat to avoid the water that was seeping in. I pressed the accelerator to the floor to get as much momentum as I could before the engine died.

Then, as if we were on a fair ride, the rear end of the Holden spun. Now the front end faced upstream. The engine revved, but there we were floating and heading downstream, sinking as we went.

The smell of the muddy water filled my nostrils, and the noise inside the vehicle sounded as if we were inside a washing machine. I was concentrating so hard on what my next move might be to worry about dying. All I could think of was getting Yvette to safe ground.

As I scanned the Orroroo side of the bank for possible places to make our break from the vehicle, the wheels caught, and we were thrown back into our seats. I yanked the wheel hard toward the upward slope, and a second later, we were out of the water.

I eased off the accelerator as we scaled the bank. After stopping at the top, I opened my door, so the water could drain out.

Yvette opened her eyes. An expression of relief was on her face, but there was a bit of tension still in her voice. "Are we still alive?"

"How are you?"

"Like I walked into a spinning propeller."

Even though I thought much the same, all I could do was flash a feeble grin.

The rain had almost stopped. I pulled the Holden forward and off the side of the road beyond the embankment. "If you open your door, you can put your feet on the floor."

I kept the engine running to dry out the engine compartment then got out and opened the back doors to survey our gear in the cargo area. My canvas duffle was good. Her bags were on top, so they weren't wet.

I glanced back at the flowing creek that appeared to have peaked and saw an entire gum tree thundering through the spot where we were less than a minute ago. I could see how people turned to prayer. As comforting as that might have been to this non-believer, my idea of comfort was to join Yvette for a drink.

Twelve

Having drained the remainder of the water from the vehicle, leaving only a thin muddy coating that marked the water level, I took the Holden back onto the paved road and headed toward the township of Orroroo. A few hundred yards ahead was a roadblock staffed by a half dozen men and women dressed in orange uniforms, black paratrooper-style boots, and safety helmets. Their uniform shoulder patch stated, 'State Emergency Services.'

One of the men, with stars on his epaulettes, waved us over. I wasn't sure what rank he was, but I presumed stars meant he was the officer-in-charge. A patch over his right breast pocket said, 'Rescue.' From the look on his face, I knew I was in trouble.

"You okay?" he asked but didn't wait for an answer. "Are you traveling alone, or are you with other vehicles?"

I could hear the crackle of his handheld transceiver with someone at the other end saying, "Standing by."

"We're fine. We're traveling alone. No one else."

He didn't respond. He pressed the push-to-talk button on the side of his radio and said, "No other vehicles."

"Roger. Out," came the radio voice.

He said, "We tried to block the other end before the storm hit, but you must have been on the road by then. You should have waited out the squall." His face was stern.

I nodded, feeling like I was addressed by a Chinese border guard.

"Not sure how you got across that creek. The middle of the road was washed out when the storm hit." He checked the interior of the cab. "I see you took on some water. You could have drowned. I should report you." He withdrew a notepad and pencil from his breast pocket.

Yvette's fingers dug into my leg. She smiled at the rescuer. "My husband was foolish. I can't believe he did that. It's *so* out of character. He's always careful. Please, I can assure you that he won't do that again—ever!" She gave me a severe glare, and poked me.

I played along. "Sorry honey, that was pretty stupid." I gave him a grin. "My apologies officer. We're tourists. Learned an important lesson back there." *But the lesson I learned is how she covers things up that are potentially embarrassing.*

He made a sucking sound with his teeth, put away the notepad then waved us on. However, before I could get into gear, he said, "Check the vehicle for snakes. They get caught up in the underbody when they get washed downstream."

We drove off. The thought of a snake hiding in a dark corner under the Holden scared me more than the thought of that tree smashing into us. *Creepy!* I wanted to say, 'Hey Yvette, do me a favor, crawl under the vehicle, see if there're any snakes,' but I couldn't, so I questioned her, "Your foolish husband?"

* * *

Luck was finally on our side. As we entered Orroroo there was a sign for a bed-and-breakfast. I turned the Holden into the driveway of the old stone house and parked under a carport that had a sign indicating 'guests.' I left the windows of the vehicle ajar to help dry the dampness. I prodded the gap with my finger, figuring that if I couldn't get my finger through, a snake couldn't get in either. I wasn't sure if that would work, but my logic seemed sound.

We checked in. I decided to inspect the underbody in the morning. Now all I wanted was to shower, put on some dry socks, and have a drink...or two.

A widow in her late sixties—Mrs. Walkley—owned the property and had converted it to a B&B when her husband died.

It was an impressive place filled with well-preserved pieces of English antique furniture. I assumed they had been in the family for a few generations. Its ambiance brought me thoughts of a Raymond Chandler's novel, *The Big Sleep*, where the action takes place in a place called *Casa de Oro*, or in English, golden house. Oro wasn't quite Orroroo, but it had a similar ring, and this house was golden in its appeal to a survivor of the misery a few kilometers back.

When we explained we had a difficult time crossing the creek, she said, "Well, you're none the worse for wear, but I think you need something to eat." She then offered us roast lamb and vegetables she had left over from her meal. We eagerly accepted. I bought a bottle of claret from a rack of wines she had on offer.

The art on the walls took Yvette's fancy, and she chatted with the hostess late into the night about their origins and the various artists, especially the Aboriginal dot paintings. These First Australians had names that were as unpronounceable as some of the Polish names in the town over from where I lived— Chicopee. I must admit, the artists' works were mesmerizing. They reflected the ancientness of the land we were traversing. I had a few drinks, and fatigue began to take hold. I said good night to the two women and fell into bed.

* * *

The morning was glorious. Blazing sun, a calm breeze, and abounding birdlife. The day was as bright as the paintings on Mrs Walkley's walls. I always knew that the world's ornithologists adored Australia as a destination for bird watching. Sitting in the garden that she created, I was treated to some of what I thought were the most spectacularly beautiful birds I'd ever seen. I had no idea what types they were, but the colors were reminiscent of a Disney film. Bright greens, blues, and reds. Mrs Walkley, a nicely presented woman with an air of grace and serenity, pointed out what she called *galahs* in a small

71

gum tree growing outside the back door. They were large pink and gray birds that hung from a branch and made a dreadful screeching sound before the flock flew off.

Her garden was a strange combination of order where there were clearly defined plantings of rosemary bushes and other herbs, interspersed with what appeared to be self-sown vegetables that had germinated from compost. Under the overhead vines were large terracotta pots filled to overflowing with herbs and flowers. A magic garden with her wooden dining table amidst the overhanging branches, garden greenery, and her six bantam chickens that roamed free.

Mrs Walkley brought out a pot of coffee and some freshly baked bread. We chatted about family. She said she had a son, who was a stockbroker in Sydney, and her daughter, a nurse with some international aid organization, working in Jordan.

When Yvette joined me in the garden, she looked as good as she did at the Hilton. I, on the other hand, felt like a piece of driftwood that needed oil rubbed into it. All I could do was to pour another cup.

Yvette sat across from me as I sipped my coffee. As I watched her hands lift her cup, it occurred to me that she wasn't *alluring* at all. She was an *illusion*, good at projecting whatever image she wanted.

"You have such an attractive garden," Yvette complimented Mrs Walkley.

"Thank you. Do you have green fingers?"

"No, the only plants I buy are cut flowers, because they are supposed to die."

I couldn't imagine Yvette kneeling in her garden, weeding.

The birdbath had been filled by the storm. It was tranquil. I asked, "Is there a garage in town where I can get the undercarriage checked for damage?" I didn't say, 'And for snakes...'

"Oh sure, call into Gibb's. He's on Second Street, near the road to Jamestown. Can't miss it."

I did the dishes while the two women finished their chat about a Pro Hart painting in the hallway.

* * *

"I was relieved to hear there was no damage to the car," said Yvette as we headed toward Hawker, the last town before Leigh Creek and Copley. After Leigh Creek, there was nothing much, but a small town called Marree 120 kilometers farther north.

I read that Marree consisted of a pub with motel facilities, a few houses, and *the last* petrol station. Once it serviced a major railhead where cattle and sheep were transported to markets in Port Augusta and Adelaide, but not anymore. The dirt road between the two was called the Oodnadatta Track, and it was for serious four-wheel drive vehicles, not rentals.

"Yep, that's good news," I responded, thinking all along that it wasn't the damage that concerned me.

The landscape was isolated. From horizon to horizon, from north, south, east, or west, there was no sign of human habitat. I couldn't imagine that anywhere could be more out-of-the-way than this, but from what I read, there was, and we were heading straight into it.

Yevette gave a satisfied sigh. "Mrs Walkley said there was a place called Parachilna not far from Leigh Creek. It sounded charming, and they serve meals. There's an art gallery there too."

I started to point out that we were behind schedule, and that if I had embarked on this mission on my own, as was originally planned, I'd be there by now. As I went to speak, tension built in my chest, and I caught myself in time. *It isn't worth it*. Instead, I turned to her, took a breath, and said, "So you want me to stop there?"

She nodded.

I gave her my best imitation of a smile.

Thirteen

I t was interesting observing the landscape this far north; it was so different from New England. Although the storm had passed, there were still pools of water on the sides of the road. I could see for kilometers, but the animals blended well with the surrounding countryside. The weather report I'd heard before we left Mrs Walkley's was for another storm in a day or so. I checked the rear-view mirror wondering if any clouds were in pursuit, but all I saw was a speck on the horizon. A vehicle of some sort, but because it was so far away, I couldn't make out its details. It surprised me because we hadn't seen a car or truck for quite some time.

In what seemed less than a minute, the car had moved up behind us at an incredible speed. I thought it might be an emergency vehicle, but there were no flashing lights. Before I could turn the Holden toward the shoulder to let him by, the car passed at what appeared to be double my speed. I noted my speedometer read one-hundred kilometers per hour. So, he'd have to have been doing 150, or 160.

Yvette gave a startled cry, and with an amazed expression, she watched the car rocket down the road, still on the other side. It made no effort to change back into the correct lane.

"Why's he driving so fast?" She had anger in her voice.

"He's not driving fast; he's flying at a low altitude."

She wasn't amused by my joke even though she claimed to be getting used to my brand of humor.

Within seconds, the car had disappeared over a rise in the road. I subconsciously slowed to ninety as I regained my composure. I went back to watching the road then I noticed a lot of debris on the asphalt. Tiny bits of something like seedpods that had been blown onto the pavement from the surrounding bushes. They made a popping sound when I drove over them. Then the 'pods' started to bounce off the windshield as more and more appeared across the roadway. Not seed pods at all—locusts. A swarm of grasshoppers darting across our path. They grew so dense I was forced to slow even more as they enveloped the four-wheel drive. The locust blanketed the road and darkened the sky. The swarm was moving from west to east, but because the insects were so thick, I couldn't make out how big flock was, or how long it would take us to pass through. The bugs impact made a drumming sound on the body of the vehicle.

"This is unbelievable," Yvette murmured. "They look little arrows flying through the air." Her face was a glassy stare.

As suddenly as the swarm appeared, it vanished. There were bug corpses all over the car. I could smell the pungent odor of cooked locust that had been diced when they passed through the fine metal mesh that formed the vehicle's radiator webbing. I switched off the ventilation fan and turned on the windshield wipers to scrape away their remains.

As the bug guts cleared, there were skid marks on the road, wide black marks that brought a sense of dread. What had caused them? Then I saw the car. It was upside-down off to the left. The wheels were still spinning. There was smoke lingering in the air from the melted tire rubber.

I pulled the Holden over, parking short of where the car left the bitumen. I stepped from the vehicle, looked around, and listened. Nothing but silence. Eerie silence.

Fourteen

My immediate thought was that he was lucky we were behind him, so we could provide aid. Yet, as soon as that thought passed, I realized he was neither lucky nor alive. The male was in his late teens, still strapped into his seat, upside-down, arms dangling and motionless. Protruding through the windshield and embedded in his chest was a fencing dropper used to support the sagging middle of a long-gone barbed-wire barrier. It must have become airborne when he left the road and flew like a spear straight into him. I reached through the smashed driver's side window, and following my training, felt his wrist for a pulse. None. His limp arm was warm and supple. It was hard to think he'd been full of life only seconds ago.

Having investigated a wrecking yard full of car accidents for insurance companies, I knew the police would want to take photos and measurements. Skid marks and tire tracks were important evidence. I didn't want to disturb what would be an investigation scene into the cause of death.

"See if your smartphone works," I yelled to Yvette as I surveyed the damage.

She made her way through the low shaggy grass that dotted the roadside. "Is he dead?"

"There's a hole in his chest with a piece of steel sticking out of it. I suspect it caused him to stop breathing." I bit my tongue, realizing my dark humor may be inappropriate. "Stay where you are. It's not a pretty sight."

"Western thought denies death. The search for Truth invites us to understand it. American Indian thought does that. A person's spirt never dies."

Her wisdom sounded a bit mystic to me. My focus was more practical. "Any phone reception?"

She held her phone in one hand and raised it over her head attempting to get better reception. She scowled. "None at all."

"Okay, we're out of range." I clasped her shoulders. "Can you cope? I need you to think clearly and go for help."

She rolled her eyes. "Of course, I can."

"Really?"

She had a quizzical gape. "American Indians view death as not an end to life, but the beginning of a deeper spiritual existence. The spirit moves through the sky, west, toward the setting sun—"

I cut her lecture short as I said, "Can you drive back to Hawker and let the authorities there know? I'll stay with him in case another vehicle comes by." I took Yvette's smartphone and snapped a photo of the car, a close-up of the license plate, and finally one of the young man inside. *That one will grab their attention.*

The teenager's eyes were black and as chilling as a Scottish lake. There was a smell of pot in the car. Strong. I suspected he had more than a few puffs.

Yvette drove away as the wheels of the upturned car stopped spinning, and I was left with the ghost of a man who would never see what life had to offer. I sat on the ground and eyed the road north and south. There wasn't anything moving in either direction.

Australia was everything I imagined: untouched, unspoiled, and majestic. Sitting on the bare ground, I added 'unforgiving' to my collection of thoughts.

I glanced at the sky. Its colors were changing as the winds tried to dissipate what was left of the storm. I was left with my thoughts about a man who never saw his end coming.

The first hour passed slowly. There was no sign of movement on the road, so my attention started to slip, time seemed to dilate, and I began dozing off. As a cloud came over and the temperature dropped, I didn't fight it. If I were conducting surveillance, I would've had a coffee. A PI can't afford to take his eyes off the target.

There have been instances where investigators have closed their eyes, even for a few minutes, and sent the whole operation down the drain. This surveillance was different. There wasn't any chance either the man or any car going past would escape my attention, even if I slept. In the cool air, that is what I did.

* * *

When I woke, it wasn't with a start. I sat up and looked around. Shadows lengthened. I was a bit disoriented at first, but then the events came back. The silence was broken only by the noise of a light breeze blowing in the distance that sounded like wind rushing through a canyon, but there was no canyon, only open space. The state of Montana was called the 'Big Sky Country.' The Flinders Ranges had to be Australia's Big Sky Country.

I checked my watch. Three hours had passed. The dead man was still there except he was now covered with flies. They filled the car. I didn't think anything could make a worse sight than him hanging upside down, but there it was, him covered with maggot-laying insects. I shook his arm. The flies buzzed, circled, then landed on him again. The last time I touched him he was warm, limber. Now he was cold and stiff.

I heard cars approaching. They came from the Hawker road. As they drew near, the markings on the lead vehicle told me they were police. The SUV had flashing lights and several antennae. Behind it, Yvette drove in the Holden. I stood and waited for their arrival. To my surprise, when the police patrol pulled up, the driver sat in the cab and stared at me. He then got out, slowly, and walked to the rear. He took a long-handled shovel off the roof rack and walked toward me. I was about to greet him when he said, "If you move, you're dead."

Shit. I read about mass murders roaming the Australian outback but wasn't told that the cops were homicidal too!

I did as I was told. I didn't enjoy the idea of being planted amongst the saltbush, so I began thinking of an escape plan.

Yvette walked up behind him. She froze with her hands over her mouth, panic in her eyes.

The cop bent over, using the shovel to reach ahead. The head of the shovel came closer and closer, but not toward me, to my right. I turned, followed its path until I saw what he was doing. The uniformed officer slid the shovel under the body of a dark-tan-colored snake and lifted it. With a flick, he catapulted it through the air into the distant scrub.

He gave me a broad smile. "I'm Detective Sergeant Lloyd Miller. Call me Lloyd." His short red hair showed through his country-style police cap. He had thick eyebrows and pale skin that would burn easily under the Australian sun.

Wooziness filled my head, and my peripheral vision faded then I couldn't see anything.

* * *

I lay on my side with my left arm under my head, and my right extended, right knee bent in the recovery position used by first-aiders. I could hear Lloyd Miller on the two-way radio in the distance but couldn't make out what was being said.

Yvette knelt on the ground in front of me, saying, "You were supposed to be protecting *me*. But I had to get help to scare away a snake for *you*."

Perhaps it was her attempt at humor. I couldn't tell. I rubbed my forehead, "Yvette, even snakes are afraid of snakes."

I could hear footsteps.

"You okay, mate?" asked the Detective Sergeant.

I sat up and greeted him, thanking him for saving me.

"No worries, mate. It was a brown snake. Common in the Ranges, its venom is really potent. I guess it was sleeping next to you trying to keep warm."

"It was sleeping next to me?" My head spun.

"Happens sometimes. They seem to be able to sense warmth, seek it out. If it bit you, it could have been fatal. Their poison attacks the nervous system and kidneys, also causing blood clotting problems. They're a nasty bag of misery." He screwed up his nose.

I had to stop thinking about it. The mental image of it was paralyzing. To change the subject, I asked, "Ambulance?"

"Yep, coming from Orroroo. Should be here soon with the State Emergency Service. They'll cut him free. The paramedics will pronounce death even though we know he is. I radioed the details to my station. They'll organize notification of next of kin. The kid's not local. He's from Port Augusta. Should have known better." He paused. "Yvette told me you're a PI. Seen a lot of traffic accidents, hey?"

"Yeah, but after the event. Not while the bodies were still inside."

"Bad luck with this one. Yvette indicated he was speeding when he hit the locust swarm."

"Speeding! If he were going any faster, he'd have traveled back in time. When you check the body, I think you'll find weed was involved."

Lloyd nodded. "There isn't anything you can do here. You can go, but I still need statements from the two of you for my report to the coroner. Yvette told me you're stopping at Parachilna for a meal. How about I see you there, so I can do the write-up?"

He started to turn then added, "When Yvette showed up at the police station, she wasn't frightened. Most people shake like a tuna on the deck of a boat. I suggest you stay the night at the Prairie Hotel, recover from this. She could have a delayed reaction." He tilted his head toward the wreck. "Keep your eye on her."

"I understand," I said, "but she's mighty tough, not the type of girl who wants to swim with dolphins."

"What?"

I shook my head. "Don't worry; we'll get rooms for tonight. I'll keep an eye on her."

He paused, appearing a bit confused then looked directly at me with the eyes of an interrogator. "There's no law against you operating here under your American PI license, but usual practice is that you check in with us before you go off making your *inquiries*. Mind if I see your license."

It wasn't a request. It was a demand. I got out my photo license and badge.

He ran his index finger across the words 'Private Investigator' on my nickel-plated shield. "What you are doing this far from home?"

I got the impression he already knew from his conversation with Yvette. I was a long way from my jurisdiction and needed to make friends, not antagonize people, especially the local law. "Her husband's gone missing. Nothing suspicious. Nothing the law needs to be concerned about." I hesitated, thinking about how much to reveal. "Matrimonial stuff," I added and winked, thinking that would convey whatever he wanted to read into it. "I located him around the Arkaroola area. I'm taking Yvette to bring him home."

He regarded me the way a collector would when examining a rare coin. "What's his name?"

"Kurt Kerslake. He's an artist. A painter. A Native American."

"Kurt Kerslake? Doesn't ring any bells. There's lots of foreign tourists up here. The Flinders Ranges is a big attraction. If he entered the country legally, then he's free to do what he wants within the limits of his visa." His voice trailed off only to peak again. "Any outstanding warrants on him?"

"Not that I'm aware of. I think he's involved with some Aboriginal group. I saw a few photos posted on a social media page. If I show you the photo perhaps you can give me a clue as to who the people are."

I retrieved my file on Kurt and thumbed through the dossier. I produced the photo of Kurt standing in front of the SUV, and waited.

His posture stiffened. "Oh, you've got an unpredictable creature there. Careful it doesn't turn on you."

"What do you mean?"

"These people are involved in a brand of Indigenous politics that..." He rolled his eyes skyward "...isn't in keeping with the wider Aboriginal community's thinking. Let's just say this group has funny ideas."

"I suspected that much. Some American Indians don't agree with government policies. They can be quite vocal. Know where I could start looking for him? There's a lot of nothing out there."

He chuckled. "A lot of nothing? You haven't seen half of it." He pointed north to the end of the mountain range that vanished into the horizon. "Wait till you get into some of those gorges and creeks. Let's talk more when I see you tonight."

I wasn't keen to stay knowing the SES were on their way. I wasn't interested in encountering that officer with the stars on his epaulettes again. We drove away, plunging deeper into the center of Australia, resuming our trip that had now been delayed by more bad luck and misfortune.

I glanced in the rear-view mirror to see the detective snapping photographs of the car and the tire marks. A moment later, I saw the lights of the ambulance that was inbound to the accident site.

Light clouds diffused the sunlight. The effect was an orange hue that glowed with the warmth of a slow combustion stove. A wonderful sight, one that occurred every day, yet there were not many people who came here to experience it. I was lucky to be among the few. It was peaceful. A feeling I hadn't experienced in a while.

Go with the flow I told myself. So, I decided to enjoy the countryside, which was like what I recalled around Nevada when I did a contract PI job in Las Vegas. I had to check on the *bona fides* for a client in Connecticut who was dating a new girl. Turned out she was a former Vegas stripper, but her previous employer referred to her as an 'exotic dancer.'

Fifteen

The settlement of Parachilna appeared in the distance, slowly at first, then as we made our way along the road, it grew. Wasn't a big place, a few houses and the Prairie Hotel, the town's centerpiece. There was a large communications tower on the south side of the township that hosted several telecommunications microwave dishes. The aerials underscored the remoteness of the location. Reminded me of a space probe that had landed on a distant planet, its antennae the only link to the civilized world.

The hamlet consisted of a disused railway siding, an old deserted schoolhouse with a few outbuildings, and a half dozen rundown, ill-maintained single-story houses. Across from the rail line that ran from Port Augusta in the south, to the Leigh Creek coalmine further north, was the Prairie. It was a renovated old stone pub with a wide veranda that had chairs and tables. At the rear was a modern architecturally designed two-story addition that housed the hotel rooms. Lemon-scented gum trees dotted the edge of the establishment, and the grounds were sprinkled with sculptures made from old corrugated iron roof sheets and odd bits of farm machinery.

Noting these, I could see Yvette instantly warm to the place. If she were a cat, she would have purred.

Her world was different from mine. She had it all—money, a career, a ten-room house, domestic help, evenings at cultural events, and her name on the invitation list to all of Boston's art openings. *Did I miss anything?* Ah, the lack of intimacy. Kurt was a drunk and seemed to be dabbling in home remedy psychopharmacology. I couldn't imagine what he might be like from his photo, but the vision of him taking her to dinner, giving her a slow massage and turning the lights down while he switched on some soft music, wasn't gelling with him hanging out in Boston bars and talking offbeat politics.

Nevertheless, I guessed she'd faked excitement in the bedroom if he could go that far. She clearly viewed him as owing her a child, and she was going after him, again, to 'do his job.'

It was hard for me to understand, but I didn't need to. She was my client, so it didn't matter what she believed if what she was asking me to do was legal and somewhere this side of being ethical.

I parked the vehicle on the opposite side of the pub's forecourt. There was a large makeshift fireplace in front of the veranda where logs fashioned into stools were arranged haphazardly. Obviously, the place to congregate when night fell.

We entered the lobby and checked in. Georgina Halliday, the owner, explained about the art gallery on the mezzanine floor then the next thing I realized, the two were wandering off, discussing some artist with a European sounding name.

"I'm so surprised how his work has moved from realism to abstractionism," said Yvette.

Art and aesthetics were beyond me.

The sun appeared to be about to crash into the earth, so I brushed away a few flies then headed back to unpack and wash for dinner.

* * *

With a fresh shirt, I took-up a position at the short-curved bar and ordered a beer. With one elbow on the polished wood and my foot on the brass rail, I stared out the door into the evening sky.

The last rays gave the view a purple glow with orange highlights. Although a different season and a different place, for an instant I thought I was sitting on the ridge back home watching the autumn colors.

A police four-wheel drive pulled into the parking lot. Detective Sergeant Lloyd Miller unfolded his lanky body and stepped out, placed his wide-brimmed hat on his head then adjusted his equipment belt. I waved to him through the open door to join me.

With good humor, he said, "Let's go outside so I can take your statement. Doesn't make for a good appearance, a cop standing at a bar while on duty."

We sat at a table on the veranda, then he took out a pile of statement forms. With his left hand, he started to fill in the details when a French tourist approached.

In broken English, he said, "I am collector of police patches. I will exchange French shoulder patch for yours."

The detective examined the patch as if examining a piece of evidence from a crime scene. "Nice. Haven't seen one of these."

"So, yes, we will have deal?" asked the tourist.

"Let me see the hotel owner, she might have a pair of scissors. I don't want to ruin my shirt."

Lloyd returned into the pub, and a minute later passed me on his way to one of the nearby houses, saying, "Got to see Blanche, the wife of the handyman. She was once a seamstress."

I picked up one of the forms and began writing my statement. I had done this more times than I cared to remember. I completed mine and wrote one for Yvette to sign. Then I saw a man I thought might be Blanche's husband approach the house. He was short, but well-built, wearing overalls and a dark blue singlet.

As the husband approached the door, it opened, and out stepped Detective Miller, his shirt off and him buckling his trousers.

"This will be interesting," I muttered.

The husband stopped in his tracks. His wife appeared at the door saying, "Pleased to help you, officer, stop by anytime."

The Frenchman ran toward the group, waving his arms, ranting something that resembled English, but it came out mostly in excited French. "That not what it looked."

Given the popular image for the French's propensity for extramarital affairs, my immediate thought was, *I wonder if he's been in a similar situation.*

I signed my statement and went looking for Yvette. The bar was full, a sea of travelers stopping for the night. I weaved my way through the crush.

Yvette was talking to the head waiter at the entrance to the dining room. She was wearing her boots with a pair of blue-black jeans tucked into them. Her silk jacket was covered with an intricate pattern of black swirls on a dark orange background. Around her neck was a single strand of burnt-orange ceramic shapes.

"He has only one table left, over there by the window. We need to eat now because they're expecting a movie crew to arrive later from their day's shooting."

"Okay, but sign this." I pushed the statement into her hand and gave her my pen. "It's your statement for the police investigation."

Her eyes narrowed.

"I've checked it. It's fine."

"Nothing about Kurt in this?"

"Nothing."

With one hand on his hip and a swagger, the waiter showed us to our table.

"Thanks Francis. I'll see to our guests," came Lloyd Miller's voice. The cop turned to us. "Sorry about that diversion, I'm a sucker for police memorabilia."

"And Blanche's husband?" I chuckled.

"Oh, that. My French friend worked some magic with his silver tongue. They're all drinking rosé on the veranda. They'll be singing soon..."

I handed him the two statements. "You'll find these to be to your satisfaction."

He thumbed through them. "I see you've written legal documents before. Many thanks, I'll be off." He walked a few paces then turned. "Safe trip."

* * *

During dinner, Yvette was light and bubbly as she discussed the art she seen. While she talked, I saw a man at another table who must have been in his late-sixties chatting-up a woman of his vintage. While Yvette's discussion of brush strokes and emphasis of color drifted past my ears, my subconscious focused on the man.

He was trying his best to be charming and dapper. In a time gone by, I thought he might have succeeded in enticing her, but physiology must have had taken hold, her libido lost along with time past. He seemed not to realize this. Or perhaps he did, yet he hoped he'd be able to defy the odds. *Surely, she can see his intent. Surely there's a spark of desire? Surely there's a smoldering ember that could be coaxed into a glow, then a flame...*

I heard her say, "Well, I have to get to Hawker. Thank you for a memorable meal."

With the smell of the wood fire being lit outside, he stood and walked her to the door. His heart must have been racing—mine would have—but it was clearly too late for words. His opportunity to say, 'Stay, spend the night,' had passed when she uttered her goodbye. Like the fighter pilot whose reactions have grown slow with age, he too seemed to have lost his edge. I sensed his dream was vanishing. In the military, the saying was,

'There are the quick and the dead.' At that moment, he must have known which category he was in.

I could relate. My dream of Faye had vanished. I was too slow. I had memories of being the school kid no one wanted to be friends with. I wondered if he experienced the same.

He smiled, said, "Thank you," and she walked out.

I watched him as he returned to the dining room and occupied himself for a few minutes viewing some of the old photographs that were on the walls. I suspected he wasn't interested in the subject matter but was buying time, so he didn't have to be seen crossing the courtyard to his room alone.

"How was your dinner?" asked Francis. While collecting our plates, he inquired, "Will you be staying long?"

I said, "No, we have to leave in the morning."

"Tell 'em you got a flat tire. Stay another night. We've got John O'Dea playing tomorrow."

Yvette smiled. "We've got to get on the road, but it's been heaven."

"Well if this is Heaven, then I must be Saint Paul." As the waiter walked away, he asked, "What more could anyone want?" and shook his hips.

Peace in the Middle East. A world without poverty, disease, or illiteracy... but before I got carried away with too many utopian thoughts, I turned to Yvette. "I'm off to my room."

"Good night. I'm going to wait for the film crew to arrive. I want to talk to them about their project."

"Sure, we're in no hurry, Copley's only a few hours up the road."

I watched her walk over to the bar. How could Kurt not be attracted? I intended to find out. Tomorrow would be the day I started my search.

Sixteen

The travel books I read at Sydney Airport said that Leigh Creek was once located thirteen kilometers further south but was relocated in 1982 when the coalmine expanded. Its population was about 500, all miners who worked in the nearby coalfields. A modern town with all the comforts of a city, except for the fact it was an oasis in the arid outback.

In comparison, the travel books depicted Copley as a speck of a town about five kilometers north. With fewer than a hundred people, it was the gateway town to the Gammon Ranges that lay to the east. That's where Arkaroola was located. The Gammons take over where the Flinders Ranges stop. Hard to believe there could be anything beyond here, but there was, including Birdsville, though it was another two days' drive.

I'm pleased he didn't decide to go to Birdsville, I tgough as Yvette and I drove through the last dried creek crossing before entering Leigh Creek. There was a large frontend loader scraping debris from the concrete ford across the creek. The forces of the swollen creek reduced everything in its flow to matchsticks. I guessed that the tumbling rocks produced an affect similar to a food processor.

The various fords we crossed before this were the same—road crews repairing the storm damage. Creek banks were washed away, and truckloads of gravel were being dumped to fill-in the erosion.

Passing through Leigh Creek, I could see it was rich and prosperous. When we arrived at Copley a few minutes later, I judged it poor from the housing standards. The mining companies that operated in the area built Leigh Creek to service their workforce. Copley didn't seem to be part of that scheme.

Dust covered the town. Surprising how soon after the rain things dried out. It was as if a blanket of fog had descended.

Only the headlights of the road trains carrying mining equipment to the sites showed through the eerie haze as they passed Copley.

There were no painted lines, yet resembling soldiers on a parade ground, pick-up trucks were all lined up, nose in, equally spaced in front of the pub. I turned the Holden into a vacant parking slot in between two Chevrolet El Camino-type vehicles. *Utes* was Australian shorthand for 'coupé utility.' A sheepdog sat in the back of one. Covered with reddish dust, she didn't move and showed no interest in us. Although my PI experience taught me to have the front of my vehicle pointing out for a quick exit, it would have drawn attention. So, I blended in with the other vehicles. We grabbed our daypacks off the back seat and headed to the front door. The pub was on the ground level with accommodations upstairs. I was relieved we had finally arrived.

We checked in and Yvette went to her room, I fetched her case. But when I returned for my duffle, there was an old Aboriginal man on a dirty white horse a few yards away. He had a flat nose, wide cheeks in a captivating black face. His eyes were deep and dark, but there was a fire in them. I recognized him as being in Kurt's Internet photo. He wore the same wide-brimmed hat, sweat stained and encircled with brightly colored plastic ear tags from cattle or sheep. Around his neck was a necklace of multi-colored old dog registration tags. He was arguing with the pub's manager.

"You'll not be bringing that animal in here," the manger stated flatly.

The old man rolled a cigarette and pulled a few stringy pieces of tobacco that stuck out the end. "He won't make the mess he did last time. I only want some grog."

"Leon, the answer is no—to both!" He shut the door to the pub, and I heard him throw a heavy latch on the inside.

Leon threw his arms up and turned to me. He pointed an accusatory finger, and in a voice that I could imagine resembled a Hollywood movie Old Testament prophet, he said, "*He* told me you'd come looking for *Him*."

I frowned. "Who told you that?"

"*He* who makes thoughts visible."

I was mildly amused by his attempt to ride his horse into the bar, but this man in variegated homemade jewelery now had my full attention. "What's the person's name?"

"He's a Wiseman. He touches the people he meets." His eyes were ablaze with excitement. "He's here to create a Paradise for all Indigenous people who've been dispossessed of their land."

"Are you taking about Kurt Kerslake?"

"He's one of us. One of our Aboriginal brothers from America."

I nodded toward the front door of the pub. "What about the grog? Was that for you or him?"

"He has suffered a thousand miseries in the fires of Hell because His land and His pride have been stolen. Grog kills His pain."

Hearing this, I thought for sure that Kurt must be suffering depression or a mood disorder. I wanted to tell Leon that alcohol was a one-way ticket *back* to that Hell, but I didn't want to get him offside. "So, Kurt drinks?"

He clenched his face into a grimace accentuating the lines already creasing his appearance. "Yeah, he drinks...but the alcohol feeds his genius. He's a dreamer! Sees things you and I can't imagine. He's going to rename your Thanksgiving Day, Invasion Day. He knows what it means not to be able to reconnect with the land for which his people were the traditional custodians."

Wow, when Leon read about the evils of drinking, he obviously gave up on reading, not drinking. Kurt's propaganda appeared to be as effective as North Korea's brainwashing program. I thought Leon might ask me to join him in lighting little candles to Kurt or dance under a mist of Holy Water.

I couldn't hold back any longer. "I don't think he's creating a dream, but I tell you he's created a nightmare for his wife." I moved closer. "Alcohol might take away the pain, but then *it* takes over. It's slow death." I gritted my teeth. "Where is he?"

"He eats electricity. No one sees him. You can only hear his words!" "What are you talking about, 'no one sees him'?"

"He's an oracle! He has enlarged our minds. Comes to us through the air like a spirit. Uses the wireless." He waved his arms in circles above his head, his flamboyant plastic bangle necklace flapping up and down. I thought he was about to conjure a lightning storm.

"The wireless?"

He pulled back on the reins and turned the horse's head down the dirt road. The beast snorted. He dug his heels into the animal's sides, and it trotted toward the edge of town. "The radio," he yelled. "You listen. Hear the Truth for yourself. Before the Age of Darkness descends!"

Leon certainly didn't need alcohol. He was intoxicated with the fantasies Kurt painted. The thought of pursuing Leon flashed through my mind but following him wouldn't have been easy. There was no place for me to conceal myself in the barren landscape. The dust the Holden would raise going cross-country would be like a beacon, signaling my location. Besides, Leon was on a horse and could go where my Holden couldn't. I recalled the difficult surveillance I did the Nevada case. *This is going to be a rural investigation job in a whole different league.*

Seventeen

"I've made a few inquiries and think I've got a lead on Kurt," I said to Yvette with some degree of professional pride.

It wasn't every day that a PI shows up at a location, and an informant walks up to *him*. I wasn't sure how he knew we came for Kurt. He might have made a lucky guess. Or, it could have been that Kurt showed him a photo of Yvette, and he recognized her when we arrived. Then again, it could've been that he was clairvoyant. Whatever the case, I was going to run with my luck. I wanted to wrap up this job.

She closed her eyes and sighed. "That's great. Can we please get him?"

"I said a *lead*, not a confirmation of his whereabouts."

She shook her head. "So, what are you waiting for? Go!"

"First, I need more information. Seems he might be broadcasting some sort of sermon. I need to talk to someone who can give me his location. Maybe there's a local art group who knows of him."

"Kurt was inspired by many artists, but recently he talked about several Australian artists. Even though they were white, they were interested in the plight of Australia's original people." She drew in a breath. "Artists such as Russell Drysdale and Sidney Nolan and Arthur Boyd. They weren't only interested in the distinctive imagery of the Australian landscape, but with righting the harm caused to Aborigines by decades of bigotry, prejudice, and misguided government policy."

Hmm, misguided government policy? Detective Sergeant Lloyd Miller's words about having an 'unpredictable creature' rang in my memory. *Politics. That's what this is about.* Religion and other ideologies, particularly politics, could easily slip from reason to emotion. Kurt appeared to have slid down a slippery

95

slope in his mind's playground. Leon was another, and so were the others who were gathered in the SUV Internet photo.

I needed to find Kurt and bring his involvement in this sorry saga to an end.

* * *

I retrieved my netbook computer from my room and set it up on a table in the bar, the only place in town that had public Wi-Fi. Now that I was within reach of Kurt, I wanted to check for any updates to his web posting. While my computer booted, I inspected the notice board. It had a copy of the dinner menu thumbtacked to it. Next to it were the usual notices about no underage drinkers being served.

I started to read the menu, but my gaze caught the edge of a flyer pinned under a pile of more recent billings advertising local bands, guitarists, and a stand-up comic. Instantly I recognized the pink shirt on a female entertainer. I held my breath, lifted the surrounding leaflets, and stared at the old poster. It *was* her!

Faye was written on the top with *Singer and Songwriter* as her calling. The date was about a year ago. I took it off the board and asked the barmaid, "Can I have this?"

Carrie, who was behind the serving counter, lifted her gaze from the newspaper she was reading. A woman with a streak of bright lavender in her hair, she had a nose ring, and several ear piercings. Although only in her early thirties, she had a skeptical appearance from what I guessed was standing off nightly offers for dates from cheap drunks. Perhaps she was waiting for the right guy, someone with warmth rather than testosterone.

"Sure, I need to clear up that board one day when things aren't so busy."

I turned around, expecting that a busload of tourists was about to enter the bar, but I was still alone.

96

I gave her a half smile. "Yeah, I know what you mean." I folded the flyer and placed it into my back pocket.

As I turned to my computer, she said, "She's a local you know. Famous. We're going to get her back one day. Sings real nice."

My heart raced. I shuffled toward the bar. "She lives in the district?" "No, lives right here in town. On the east side of the rail line."

I needed a pretext to see her. "I'm a big fan of country music, might get her to autograph this for me. How do I find her?"

"Cross the train line at the old station platform, head up Harris Street. It's the house with the beer keg for a letterbox. You'll know it when you see it."

I've had a lot of clouds in my life, but occasionally one was accompanied by a rainbow. I was off to find the pot of gold.

So, I ran my Internet check on Kurt, found nothing had changed, and shut down the computer. I pushed opened the door to the street, leaving Carrie with my netbook and the scent of stale beer.

* * *

I could barely hear the sound of my footsteps as I hurried across the train line. There was a flock of Sulphur-Crested Cockatoos making a loud racket in one of the eucalyptus trees that dotted the deserted station terminus. There were so many of them they looked like Christmas baubles on a pine tree. Their dark black eyes, distinctive beaks, and yellow crests gave them the appearance of uniformed musicians in a marching band. Their sound came to a crescendo as an Aboriginal teenager gave me a wave as he rode past on his BMX bike. The birds then took to the air in cascade. A moment later, it was quiet.

No green lawns, no lush shade trees, and ill-maintained roads, most of which were dirt. She did say the annual rainfall was ten inches. The houses seemed to me to be of the style built by government as a public housing project. Housing for those who had little hope of owning a place without help. Dogs, thin but muscular, wandered through the streets hoping to exchange a pat for food. Almost a ghost town.

I could see Faye's house from several houses away. It was a standout with the aluminum beer keg that was crafted into a mailbox.

The house was in better condition than its neighbors but built in what might be called 'project homes' style. It looked as if she tried to maintain it the best she could on a singer's wages. I stood in front, read the sign on the mailbox—'43 Third Street,' and under it in a fancy script, 'My Comfort Zone.'

I mumbled, "She was being literal."

She lived in a pale-yellow house made from sheets of fibrocement with a corrugated galvanized iron roof. There were three steps leading to a veranda under a wide awning that encircled three sides of the house. No doubt the overhang was to help keep the intense sun out during the summer.

There was an old two-seater sofa on the veranda. That made me smile. I could picture her sipping a cool mojito and singing country ballads with her new guitar.

The door was open with a screen to keep the flies out. I knocked. I could hear her voice call out from somewhere inside, "What?"

"I hear you need a man who can fix things."

Silence. A long uncomfortable pause. I wasn't sure what was happening. Then came her puzzled words from the back of the house, "Who's that?"

"My visa's good for three months. I can do a few jobs in the meantime."

There was a scream of delight as she came running to the door. The sound of her feet echoed on the polished pine floorboards. I stepped aside as she pushed the wooden screen door open, slamming it against the outer wall, chipping flakes off the already peeling paintwork. She threw her arms around me.

"Can't believe it's you. How'd you find me?" She stopped and pushed me back a little, holding my shoulders. "You some kind of stalker?" She laughed. Her smile was welcoming. She shook her head. "I knew you weren't into real estate. Those blokes always hand-out business cards."

I swung my arm in an arc sweeping the horizon. "I think the countryside is spectacular."

"I have no fear of falling overboard here."

* * *

Sitting on the veranda sofa, I explained about being in Australia and trying to find Yvette's husband.

Although she made some remark about Yvette busying herself arranging her shoes according to heel height, it didn't take her long to become intrigued with my manhunt. She suggested that we talk to Doris Wooragee. Faye suggested that 'Auntie,' as she called her, would know what was happening in Copley. "Half of the district is related to her, and the half that isn't is related to the half that is."

I got the picture. Auntie Doris Wooragee was the person to talk to. Before we got up to go, Faye said, "Tell me about your wife. You must miss her."

"I do. When she died—" I stopped because my eyes started to mist. "When she was told it was terminal, she gave up on radiation and chemo. The disease wouldn't let her eat. She could hardly drink. When she did, she vomited. She developed a blood clot and never regained consciousness. I wasn't there to say goodbye."

"I'm sorry," Faye said and took my hand. Her strong grip emitted warmth; her skin was soft.

I composed myself. "Don't be. Her passing is part of life's journey."

"I'm sorry about what I said on the plane—you know, about not caring about you losing your wife. I thought you were looking for a bit of fun."

She reached down and with the same sturdy grasp that she first shook my hand; she grabbed me by the crotch. "I understand that in your line of work you need to make up stories to get information. Don't ever to do that with me. Never lie to me about us. If you do, I'll take the rotary hoe out of my shed…" and she gave my manhood a squeeze.

"You'll never have to do that, because I'll never lie to you."

"Truth is more important to me than anything." She moved her face close. Her lips brushed mine, teased them, and then caressed them. A deep tender kiss followed.

Faye was weaving a spell, and I was under its power.

"I want to be with you," she said.

Eighteen

Her bedroom was large with high ceilings and two big windows. There was a ceiling fan, but no air conditioner. A door to the right led to an *en suite* bathroom that had a small shower alcove. It was all hospital white. I doubted that it had ever been renovated. The room was of the no-frills variety but decorated in colorful soft furnishings.

"I'm going to use the bathroom," she said and disappeared carrying a towel.

I opened the windows and heard the shower running. I leaned against her writing table that was opposite the bed and surveyed the room.

The water suddenly stopped, and I heard her call out, "If you can get away from 'Imelda' tonight, we should eat at Donna's. I can introduce you to some of my friends."

Faye Bellcroft appeared at the bathroom door in a one-size-fits-all bathrobe and tendrils of damp hair. Even without shoes, she was tall. Her frame was slight and angular, legs long and smooth. Without hesitating, she stood in front of me, undid the terrycloth belt, and let the robe fall from her shoulders. Her skin was well toned. She smelled of a soft floral fragrance. Her rosebud breasts screamed out to be caressed. My heart raced. She stepped closer, placing the side of her face on my chest, wrapping her arms around me, and clenching my bottom as she pulled herself into me. Her thighs parted, and she brushed herself against my erection.

She was tender, warm, and comforting. I missed being held in a woman's arms. I needed this.

She let the robe drop to the floor, bunching around her feet as she unzipped my fly. Her strong fingers reached in to expose me. With a gentle rocking motion, she rubbed me up-and-down against her zone. Her breathing deepened. So, did mine. I smelled *her* over the fragrance. My senses were in overdrive. I wanted her. Regardless, I could see she wanted me to provide for her. At that instant, I had a vision of a woman drowning in deep shadowy water, reaching up for help. I was the one she was reaching for. I needed to be there to save her from the dark depths of her loneliness.

I ran my hands along the curve of her hips and guided her movements as she picked up rhythm. My hands moved with the moist skin of her waist, up-and-down. She was like a dancer, experiencing the exhilaration of a bass beat, and for a long time she rocked rhythmically, all the while pressing her face against my chest. She finally shuddered in quiet rapture then she slowed and stopped.

I kissed her neck and asked, "Are you okay?"

She lifted her head and smiled. "I've got a cramp in my foot." We both laughed. "You don't know how much I needed that. I can't recall the last time I had sex." She held my hands, and her eyes beamed. "Thanks, you're so kind, but I can't leave you in that condition." With perspiration glistening in the vee between her breasts, she led me to her bed.

After, I lay next to her, experiencing the gentle breeze on my skin. I drifted in a world of thoughts, comfortable in her presence. She had saved me from the same darkness.

Nineteen

A pair of galahs watched us from the top of a gum tree, while we strolled through the township.

"So, we're going to see your aunt?" I asked.

"Doris Wooragee is an elder in the Aboriginal community. 'Auntie' is polite term of endearment for an Aboriginal woman," Faye explained.

At the intersection, we turned north.

"I think I understand, my wife—" I hesitated, gaining the courage to say her name, "Ellen, was an anthropologist. I know a bit about kinship and the social structures of Indigenous tribes. Mainly from listening to her and her academic colleagues discuss their research during dinner parties and weekend get-togethers."

She regarded me with more than a bit of confusion. "So why me? I'm an entertainer. Been around a bit, had some low times. People might think of me as 'damaged.' Why are you interested in me?"

At that moment, a sandy colored dog wandered up to us and sat in the dust. We stopped, and Faye greeted him, "Hello Barney, what's up?" He regarded us and, like the wipers on a windshield, used his tail to sweep slow semicircles in the dirt. We started up again, picking up our pace. The dog fell into step, leaving a small cloud of dust to settle.

I reached for her hand. "That's what makes you attractive. You're honest. Easy to talk to. I enjoy what we discuss. We share the same thoughts. You have ambition, and you're going back to study." I paused. "And, for the record, we're all damaged in one way or another."

Her muscular fingers gripped me. "You have a warm heart."

103

No matter what she confessed, it wouldn't have diminished my feelings for her. "I like you. A lot."

She smiled, but I had changed the subject before my heart took over and I made some awkward comment about love. Pointing to Barney, I said, "Hey, won't his owner miss him? On my way over, I saw a few dogs wandering around."

"Yea, Barney has an owner. The others too, but this town's one backyard." She pointed to the skyline. "You see there are no suburbs; we're a small community. We take care of each other and each other's pets." She tilted her head. "You have a family? Kids I mean."

"I've three children—a son twenty-four and twin daughters twenty-three."

"They aren't kids. They're adults. They live with you, at home?"

"My son's a lawyer, who works in Chicago. He practices business law. Sounds boring to me, but he loves it and the big city life. One of my daughters is a civil engineer. She works in Canada as a junior on a gas pipeline project that runs south through the Yukon Territory. The other daughter is at med school and works part-time in gene research at a local clinic,' helping to design drugs that target blood diseases."

"You must be proud. If I had kids like that, I'd be boasting to everyone. I can't have children. I've got problems with my uterus." Her gaze moved toward the sky, as her words came slowly, "I wanted to know the love of family. I've never married, but I have 'offspring' of sorts. My children are my songs."

I could hear the rawness in her voice.

"Like your children, I hope my 'kids' will inspire people, make a better world. We'd all want to leave our DNA to the future, but I'm not able, so I do it through my songs."

"I'm sorry."

104

"Don't be. As a wise man once told me, 'it's part of life's journey'." She took my hand. I sensed her inner softness.

I said, "It's okay to cry. It helps heal the heartaches of life."

She rubbed her eyes with the back of her hand. At that moment, I could see the image of her waking up on the plane, massaging her eyes with the blanket.

"I'm comfortable with you," I said and meant it, but it was a coward's way of avoiding the words I wanted to say. Words I hadn't uttered to a woman in a long time—*I love you*. I hesitated. I wasn't sure if that would be too much, too soon. Might weigh her down. My discussions with Sophie hadn't anticipated I'd be at this point anytime soon, so I changed the subject. "Have you lived here long?"

"All my life. Born at Peterborough. You know where that is?"

"Yeah, saw it on the map, southeast of Orroroo."

Her face beamed. "Yeah, that's right. Anyway, Mum and Dad moved here soon after I was born. Dad worked at the coalfield. He was an electrician. Mum was at home. They both passed away in my last year of high school. They smoked. Auntie Doris was a great support during those times. I didn't finish school, so she encouraged me to use my musical talents."

"Ever thought of singing in the big cities?"

"Did a few tours of the capital cities. Don't care for them. I preferred Tamworth, the music festival. Played there every year. I haven't missed a show. That's where I got the gig on the cruise ship. An agent signed me up." She blushed. "Won't be doing that again."

"No, I should say not." Now it was my turn to squeeze her hand. I thought back to the autumn leaves I left behind. "People need to learn how to flourish in the garden where they've been planted."

"How true. My life's here. I want to study to become a teacher now." She stared directly at me. "And what about your life? Is your life about tracking down missing persons?"

"Has been, but I quit my job with the PI firm I was working for. Now I'm doing freelance cases. I'm searching for a new garden to establish roots." I wanted to say, *I can envisage a life here, with you*, but I didn't.

She stopped me and drew me into her arms. We kissed. It was spontaneous. A closeness I hadn't experienced with a woman since Ellen's passing. *How could this be happening to me?* It was as though a shaft of light had broken through the clouds of loneliness and was shining on me.

Those thoughts were interrupted when something rubbed against my leg. I glanced down. It was Barney. He was sitting and swishing his tail back and forth through the dirt, staring at the two of us as if to say, *feed me*.

Twenty

"He's not like the others. Has manners. Speaks well, sounds intelligent," said Auntie Doris. She reached out, placed a hand on my shoulder. "He's a keeper if I ever saw one."

Faye poked me in the ribs with her finger, "He's a Renaissance man."

Doris Wooragee was a sturdy woman with a disarming voice. "Well, well, I do think you're right. Come in. Sit. I've got the kettle on. Peppermint tea?"

I had the suspicion that Auntie's charm might have been a sign I was in for a cross-examination that would make a polygraph session more appealing.

I peered out her living room window at her front yard. Auntie's yard resembled an Aladdin's cave of mechanical junk. Old, broken, and disused farm equipment, car parts, diesel engines, and car bodies lay here and there. I guessed she was in her late seventies, but she could have been older.

She told me she and her sister were educated at a Christian school in Adelaide. She received her degree from what she called 'Teacher's College' where she majored in English literature. She had worked as a teacher with Aboriginal children before she retired. Now she let the local boys use her yard to repair their cars. She said it helped stop them stealing parts.

"He's so much better than the others. Those 'musos' were nothing but no-hopers," she said to Faye from the kitchen, loud enough for me to hear.

People do things for reasons, so I assumed she wanted me to note what she was saying.

"I knew you'd bring home a keeper one day."

Faye Bellcroft blushed. "Auntie, he—"

"Oh, I'm sorry dear; I assumed he was someone you met on the cruise. Silly me, I hope I wasn't out of line."

I got the sense she didn't care. She was no doubt fishing for information.

"Not at all," I said as we followed her into the kitchen. I tried to gather the courage to say, 'I want to be the man she keeps,' but when I glanced at Faye for a sign of how best to describe our relationship, she wasn't looking back. Perhaps she was wondering what I'd say and, I suppose, pondering how I'd define our budding intimacy.

The issue was a potential double-edged sword. If I said we were a couple, and she didn't agree, I'd be in trouble. If I said we were friends, and she was expecting more, I was in trouble. I thought about Corey sleeping in the guest room because he didn't get Beth's birthday present right.

So, I split the difference. "We're close friends."

"Close friends. I see." She emphasized the word *close* as she brought a pot of tea to the table. "Show me your hands."

Trying to control them from shaking, I leaned against the aluminum edge of her cream Formica top table, held them out."

She ran her thumbs over my palms, rubbing the lines several times. Then she squinted at me. "You don't smoke or gamble. You drink, but in only in moderation. You don't own a racing yacht or a private plane. And, you certainly don't throw extravagant parties or womanize."

My shoulders straightened, my chest puffed-out. "You can tell all that from my palm?"

From across the table, Faye said, "Nooo! She's not a gypsy. However, she knows what I'm not interested in in a man."

The two women giggled.

I'm sure my face turned red.

"So, what brings you to me?" asked Auntie Doris. She poured from the old tea pot that was in contrast to Yvette's bone china.

I explained that I was a PI and told her about the situation with Yvette's husband. I explained about how Faye and I met, my mission to find Kurt Kerslake, and my information that indicated he was somewhere near Arkaroola. I said I needed to bring him back.

She listened intently and agreed to help. She went on to warn me that the small group of people with Kurt were crazy.

"Crazy?" I asked.

"Ya, you can spot them at the car wash. They're so obvious."

"How do you mean?'

"They're the ones on motorcycles."

She and Faye burst into laughter. Must have been a local joke. Their amusement was infectious; made me laugh. The three of us sat chuckling.

Doris Wooragee was a woman full of grace. She leaned across the kitchen table, placed her wrinkly black hand on mine. "I would like you to be the one she keeps too. But you're going to have to be more than close friends."

This was a woman of compassion, who instilled confidence with an almost mystic perspective.

I wanted to say, *I want to have a life with Faye*, but I couldn't. There was something inside holding me back.

Auntie changed the subject. "The bunch this Kurt fellow is tied up with is out past Mount Rose, squatting on the old Yankaninna Station. It's about halfway to Arkaroola."

"Thank you. That's helpful."

"Not so fast, young man. There's only one track in, and you won't get past Mount Searle Station. There's a sobriety patrol and they have tall, skinny mates."

"Skinny mates?" I asked.

Faye explained, "They're an Aboriginal women's group who set up a picket line to prevent alcohol from getting into the traditional hunting lands beyond the track tourist's use. They have shotguns."

I turned to Auntie. She raised her eyebrows in confirmation.

Faye continued, "The cops don't want to know what happens out there because they know the problems alcohol causes in Aboriginal communities. They leave the women alone and let them maintain the picket. White men mean trouble. They sell grog to Aborigines, so they're not welcome."

My newfound enthusiasm for finding Kurt Kerslake disappeared the way water runs down a drain.

Auntie bent as if she was about to reveal the darkest secret of her past. Not knowing what to expect, I held my breath. In a low voice, she said, "They're only loaded with rock salt. If you get hit, you'll be the sorest bloke this side of the Strzelecki Track, but you aren't going to die."

Faye's head snapped around. "How do you know?" She seemed genuinely confused at this revelation.

In a hushed tone, Auntie continued, "Because I do the reloads. Don't either of you speak a word of this. The girls bring me their cartridges. I take the shot out and replace it with rock salt." She winked.

I glanced at Faye, and she at me. There was relief on her face.

"Mind you," Auntie went on, "you'll have one sorry arse if any of those girls pulls the trigger on her twenty-gauge." She raised her hand and made an outline of a handgun with her index finger and thumb. With a sudden jerk, she slammed her thumb over as if it were the hammer of a gun being fired. "Bang!" she bellowed.

This time no one laughed.

Though, I was still relieved. I thought she might have said it was kryptonite in those cartridges.

Twenty-One

I could hear the sound from the television over the noise of the crowd. There seemed to be a large throng assembled in the front bar of the Copley pub. The sounds greeted me some distance down the street. I pushed the door open and stepped inside. The lights were brighter than in an American bar and there was more socializing. There were men in groups, talking and joking. There were also a few women, who didn't try to cover up their features.

Yvette was there at a small table off to one side. She was by herself, drinking white wine from a long-stemmed glass. It wasn't crystal and, I suspect, not to her liking. I wondered how she would cope if we had to stay here more than a few nights. She was staring at the TV news. Some minor drama was being reported from a nondescript place somewhere in the world as if it was going to change the course of history. *Maybe it would...*

I walked over to her table, "Have you eaten?"

She looked up with a frown. "Yeah, a steak. I needed a chainsaw to cut it. I think they eat buffalo out here."

"Might be why the dining room is called 'The Tough'." I pointed to the sign over the entrance to the dining area.

There were no beautiful people in beautiful clothes in this pub. No inspiring artworks on the walls. Only mine workers dressed in tradesmen's clothes and above the bar a series of portraits of local men, who must have done something important. Perhaps bowled-out a rival cricket team or sheered the most sheep in a season. Maybe even bred a bull that won a prize in an agricultural show, or whatever it took to be a legend in these parts. The gathered folk appeared to have come straight from work or drove in from their farming properties if that was what they were called. *Farming* seemed such an odd term out here. It was so dry I couldn't imagine anything growing. Maybe that's why they were called *stations*.

"Where've you been?" she asked.

Her expression was hard. I could tell she didn't enjoy being here. I could see why. Most of the men still had their hats on. Their boots were the high-sided leather type, rugged. There was a young woman, mid-twenties, with short-cropped hair and tattoos. She was standing with a few men with whom I assumed she worked at a mine. She wore the same style work clothes. She stirred the ice in her drink with her middle finger and then placed it in her mouth, sucking on it. The men seemed to enjoy the display.

I guessed it wasn't the type of gathering Yvette would have chosen to attend. Certainly, not the type of guests she'd invited to one of her gallery openings.

"I ran into the woman I sat next to on the Sydney flight. Had no idea she lived here. Anyway, we had dinner at Donna's Café on the next corner over. We should eat there tomorrow." Yet, I knew Yvette wouldn't appreciate that any better.

She didn't seem to be interested. She appeared to be taking in the scene. Suited me because I was still working-out how I'd get past the sobriety patrol. I wanted to present her with a plan rather than excite her with more leads.

Then a voluminous, brunette backpacker brushed slowly against my back as she walked past. She had a sleeveless singlet that was two sizes too small. Her breasts bulged through the yellow fabric as if someone had over-inflated a balloon. I tried not to notice her cleavage, or her tight cut-off jeans that barely covered her bottom. I pictured her as a spider seeking a fly. I turned away. The way men stared at her with their expressionless faces said more than any expression could.

A group of four men sat at the bar exchanging glances at Yvette. In between they smirked and whispered short utterances under their breath. I knew something was up when the one with a two-day-old stubble, earring, and shaved head paraded over. He held the back of his hand to his mouth and belched before he leaned forward. "I didn't know angels could fly this low."

Yvette turned slowly, glared at him, and in a voice that could freeze Hell, asked, "What's your name?"

He grinned. "Viktor Gjeka." He threw a glance to his friends.

His friends snickered and the one with a tuff of hair on his chin raised his beer as if to say, 'Keep going mate, you're in!'

Yvette touched her hand to her chest, "My gosh, so *you're* the guy whose name's written on the wall of the women's restroom. Says you've got a needle-dick, and you hump ferrets."

His jaw dropped. He stood stunned with his mouth gaping. His friends turned away, went back to watching TV. He was on his own.

"Why's your mouth open?" she demanded. "Did you forget your lines or are you trying to catch flies?"

He appeared stunned.

"Listen, you're pretty short. Why don't you think about dating Barbie instead?"

Ouch. She's heartless. If she had put on perfume, it would've been Agent Orange.

One of his friends at the bar yelled, "Give it a rest," motioning for him to re-join them.

"Where'd you pick up those snappy comebacks?" I asked.

"Boston bars, while searching for Kurt. He spent a lot of time in them, when he wasn't painting. I had to fend off the drunken predators."

The bartender splashed vodka into someone's glass. Someone else turned down the TV and cranked up the music. It was a cover of *Spooky*, a slow jazz rendition. I didn't know the

114

band. Yvette grabbed my arm, stood me up, threw her arms around me, and held me loosely. As we danced, true to form, she led.

"Do you think I was too tough on him?" she whispered as we swayed to the beat.

I shook my head. "He's proof dinosaurs still roam the Earth."

Soon the song changed to something that sounded as though it was played with an electrified strand of barbed wire, so we went back to the table.

"Thank you." She yawned and finished her drink. "See you in the morning."

As she walked to the exit that led to the upstairs hotel rooms, Viktor hollered out, "Don't forget your broom."

"You're lucky I didn't release the flying monkeys," she replied without turning her head.

On the other side of the bar room was a casually dressed guy. He had a spiky haircut and a neatly pressed shirt. He was sitting at a table by himself, and I could see he was eyeing Carrie. He seemed too shy to approach her.

The four at the bar turned their drunken attention to his hair. "What's happened, mate? Why it's all standing up? Did ya ride in the back of the truck with the dog?"

I asked Carrie for a Cuban rum and walked over to the spiky haired guy. "Don't let 'em worry you. They're only visiting the planet." I stuck my hand out and introduced myself.

In a reserved voice, he replied, "Harold Briggs." He was medium height, not much of a build, but his clean appearance set him apart from the work gear the miners wore.

Viktor Gjeka and his friends were still mouthing sarcastic remarks in Harold's direction.

I turned to face Viktor. "Hey, what's with *your* haircut?"

The room went quiet. Eyes glanced at Viktor, then at me. I got the sense he might have taken it from a woman, but not a man.

He stood, placed his beer on the bar, and menaced me with his stare. In a measured voice, he said, "What did you say?"

I muttered, "You can't scare me, I've lived with two daughters," and I pointed, "Your bald head. You trying to look like Uncle Fester?"

The room erupted in laughter. The blonde backpacker rushed over to him, ran her hands across his head, bent it forward, and laid a kiss on his shiny dome. Seconds later the two were exiting the bar, his hand pawing her bottom. The atmosphere became more relaxed.

I turned to Harold. "So, what do you do out here?"

"I'm a radio technician, originally from Sydney, but been working in the bush for almost two years. Only been with El Dorado Mineral Exploration for a few weeks, though."

"Don't suppose you know many people in town?"

"No. Most of the blokes don't talk to me. Thanks for getting Viktor off my back. If I knew he was going to be here, I wouldn't have come. He's done this to me ever since I arrived."

"You never have to apologize for who you are, and never to his type. If you let bullies push you around, there's no stopping them. Appeasement never works."

Poor guy, nothing worse than trying to fit in when you're a little different. He seemed pleasant enough. Then it dawned on me, *a radio technician!* "Know anything about CB radios?"

His eyes sparked with excitement. "Sure, why?"

"I'm trying to find a guy who uses the CB to broadcast–" I hesitated, fumbling for a polite descriptor "–*speeches* to the Aboriginal community."

116

"Oh, you mean 'The Voice.' Not sure what his handle is, but that's what I call him. He's a Yank. Hear him now and then on my radio scanner. I heard him on my way here tonight."

Herold Briggs was a nerd. As the saying goes, a nerd is a four-letter word who can command a six-figure income. This guy was smart. I could tell. I needed him on my team.

"You know him? I'm trying to locate him, want to talk to him, person-to-person, not on the air. Can you help me?" I didn't want to appear too keen, but the odds were stacking up against me now that I knew there was a blockade.

"Sure, but can't say I understand what he's saying." His face flushed a little with awkwardness. "I don't mean about his Yankee accent. I enjoy the Yank accent." He glanced up at me. "What I mean is, what he says doesn't make sense. It's like listening to an Icelandic exchange student. I can only understand every third word."

I don't usually flash my PI license. Some people think it's pretentious, but others see it an emblem of serious work. I got the impression Harold was a serious guy. I slipped my black leather ID wallet out of my pocket, opened it and slid it across the table surreptitiously, positioning it in front of him, making it a bit of a show.

"I'm a PI, here to locate that guy and bring him back to the States. The woman I was with earlier is his wife. She's quite concerned." I pointed my finger to the side of my head. "He's not well and needs treatment. Can you help me locate him?"

He glanced at the ID, appeared to read the details, and pushed it back. "Massachusetts?" He rested his back against the chair. "The Bee Gees wrote a song about Massachusetts. All about people who are trying to get back to the place they left."

I said, "He needs to get to the place he's left, with the woman he's left behind." I leaned forward and slid my chair closer. "The police aren't involved. This is a private inquiry. My work is discreet. Can you keep a secret?"

Twenty-Two

His face was barely visible under the green illumination of the LCD screen of his radio scanner. I don't think anyone could have seen us sitting in the cab of his ute, but I wasn't concerned. I wanted to hear his voice, to put some substance to the man in my dossier photo. I needed to get a sense of his personality; to understand the man who walked out on a woman and a life that others could only aspire to.

The screen scrolled with numbers as the device searched the ether, so fast it was hard to distinguish the digits. Like the jackpot on a poker machine, the stream of numbers stopped, and a string of figures appeared on the screen: 477.375.

Harold's finger pointed to the digital display. "Listen. He's on UHF channel thirty-nine."

Then I heard him. As clear as if he were next to me, his voice came through the vehicle's speakers. I could see what Harold was talking about, and it was a slow rambling sermon reminiscent of historical footage I once saw of Fidel Castro addressing the people of his captive nation. That speech went on for hours, and basically said the same thing as Kurt—nothing.

"Where is he?" I asked.

"For that, we need to do some calculations."

From a storage box in the tray compartment of his *ute*, Harold got out a small antenna that resembled a TV aerial. He connected it to his scanner with a length of a black coaxial cable then said, "See that set of bars to the right of the display? That's the signal strength, similar to what's on your cell phone. More bars mean it's a stronger signal. I'll pan the horizon; you tell me when it reads the strongest."

Pointing his antenna at the skyline, he pivoted from left to right. Like a radar operator searching for an hostile aircraft, Harold Briggs was seeking Kurt's radio signal.

"There! It's strongest there," I told him.

He took out his smartphone, called up some app, and said, "Remember this bearing," then rattled off a series of coordinates.

I noted them on a pad.

"Okay, we need at least one more point to triangulate his position. Two will be better. Let's drive down the track toward Arkaroola, see what we can figure out."

We drove out of the town, east along the gravel track that eventually ends at what the travel books I looked at in Sydney described as some of the most rugged granite peaks in all the Flinders Ranges. According to the books, there are mysterious waterholes that were formed by the rains and natural springs.

As we drove, he talked fast, as if he'd had a couple of espresso coffees. He told me about how Kurt was operating on a simplex frequency. If he were operating through the repeater at Mount Rose, we would have had to listen to him on his input frequency. He said, "People often get repeater frequencies mixed-up, because they forget about the offset."

I wasn't sure what he was talking about but got the gist. I was confident that if I were to find Kurt Kerslake, it would because of Harold.

We drove for a couple of kilometers, and Harold did his direction finding scan again while I monitored the signal strength meter.

"Okay, we have two compass bearings. If we plot them on a map at the point where they intersect, that's where he'll be. Because I'm only using a handheld Yagi beam, I want one more bearing, to be sure."

I was happy with that. I wanted to be sure too. We drove a few minutes more and repeated the procedure.

"Now, I need a map to plot the vectors. I can use Google maps, but I'll have to get my laptop," he said.

I said, "I've got one back at the pub. Carrie stowed it behind the bar. I can connect to the Wi-Fi there."

* * *

Parked outside the hotel, Harold's face was illuminated by the colors of the Internet map on the screen of my netbook. I read him the coordinates for the first two bearings we took, and he said, "He's at a place the locals call Goat Canyon. Read me the third, and I'll confirm it."

I rattled off the numbers, and before I finished, he shouted, "I knew it. Goat Canyon. He's there for sure."

He twisted the screen so I could see. He pointed to a feature on the map that had the appearance of a ramp—a long sloping hill that was bordered on the other three sides by steep cliffs. Creek beds ran along the feature's base.

"See, it's a perfect spot. High and in the clear for a good UHF signal, flat on top for camping, and inaccessible except by foot, and only from this direction."

Then it dawned on me. "Or horseback." That's why Leon was riding. He was supplying Kurt with provisions by the only way to get across that creek, a horse. I started to make a few notes on my smartphone.

"Here, do you need a light?" Harold asked then he produced a small battery-operated light.

"No, I'm fine. I can read in the dark."

He frowned. "How can you do that?"

"I went to night school."

He was the first person to laugh at that joke.

I asked, "How do I get there?"

Harold traced the route on the screen with his finger, pointing out that there was only one road for me to travel. He said the mountains and gorges prevented anyone from getting through any other way unless they were walking, or as I had suggested, on horseback.

When his finger traced across a place called Mount Searle Station, I made a mental note. After he finished his excited tour, I said, "See this place? 'It's a problem."

"No, you shouldn't have a problem. The track through there's fine."

"Not the track. There is a sobriety patrol positioned at that point to stop alcohol getting through."

He squinted and rubbed the back of his neck.

"I have a plan. I need your help. Think you can do it?"

He began to babble, "I always wanted to do something legendary. The most exciting thing I've done in my trade was when I climbed a twenty-meter tower to install a microwave dish. Tonight's been the best time I've had. I've used my radios to track down a fugitive!"

I didn't want to correct him and tell him Kurt was an errant husband, so I embellished the truth. "Well, I'll tell you straight, if you assist me, you'll be putting yourself in harm's way. Those women at Mount Searle Station are armed with shotguns. I have intelligence that tells me they'll shoot."

He licked his lips, gulped. "I've never done anything like Michael Westen in *Burn Notice*."

"There's little chance that you'll meet Fiona Glenanne on this mission, but are you interested?"

He hunched his shoulders. "Sure, but what if I let you down? I couldn't even deal with Viktor."

"Sometimes in the game of life, it seems as though the umpire has turned the other way. It's not about being *the* best. It's about you being *your* best."

He started to bite his fingernails.

"It's up to you, but if you miss this opportunity, regrets can pile up with the books you never read."

He clutched the steering wheel. "We're not going to do anything that's illegal."

"It doesn't matter because this mission won't exist."

His eyes lit up. "We'll need radios and cyphers and—"

"Whoa, we're not talking about safeguarding NATO's missile launch codes. We only need a simple set up so we can find this bloke."

He nodded, punched in a few numbers on the keypad of his scanner, and I heard a weather report. It was an automated information message generated by a metallic computer voice.

I cocked my head. "What's that?"

Harold said it was being broadcast from the airstrip at Leigh Creek. "Heavy rains on the way. We've got to go in the morning."

Twenty-Three

I had put down my coffee cup on the table when I saw Yvette enter the dining room for breakfast. Although the hotel didn't have a gym, she was dressed for a run.

"Thought I'd have some yogurt and juice before I did a lap of the town," she said. "Surprised to see you here."

"I'm on my way out. Received some information that might prove useful in locating Kurt."

Without hesitating, she said, "I'm coming."

Before I could say anything, I heard Harold's voice through the speaker/mic of the handheld transceiver he gave me. "Zulu Prime, this is Zulu Bravo."

"Who's that?" she asked.

"He's my man in Havana."

"Oh. You've read too many thrillers."

Harold's voice came again. "Chocks away old boy. Got to go and beat Jerry so we can all be home before Christmas."

Yvette screwed up her face. "What?"

"It's a saying. From the Second World War. British pilots were supposed to have said it before they left on their missions over Europe." I pressed the push-to-talk key on the side of the radio. "Wheels up."

"Come again?" she asked.

"It's our counter-sign to start the operation." With a whisper of mirth, I added, "I'm thinking about calling it *Operation Ramrod*."

She ignored me. "Give me fifteen minutes to change."

My attempts to get her in checkmate have so far failed, but this tactic was going to give me victory. "Sure, I'll be waiting outside by the vehicle."

When she went upstairs, I ducked out the door and met Harold in the parking area. "We'll go in two vehicles. For redundancy purposes."

I lied; I had a plan for Harold. He wasn't coming all the way. There were to be no witnesses if I had to bring Kurt back kicking and screaming. Yvette could deal with him at that point.

* * *

Minutes later, I checked the rear-view mirror and only saw dust. I knew by the time Yvette returned it would have settled, and she would have no idea where we went. After a few kilometers, I radioed Harold. "Pull over."

We got out, and I had him help me collect a few old cans that lay amongst the remnants of a blown tire, a broken radiator hose, and bits of an old fan belt that were strewn along the side of the track. It was all a testament to how unmerciful the countryside was on vehicles and the people who drove them.

We inserted a few stones into each can and put them on the floor on the passenger's side of my vehicle. I was determined to bring Kurt Kerslake back, and if I had to play dirty, I was going to.

Harold was in the lead again when we turned north off the main track onto a narrower dirt path. It had a handmade sign for Mount Searle Station.

The path was deeply rutted. There was a gate in the fence with a sign saying, 'shut the gate,' but it had rusted in the open position, along with the Tin Man in the *Wizard of Oz*.

When we cleared the crest of a ridge, Harold's brake lights came on. I got out and approached his ute.

He pointed. "Two hundred meters ahead, there's the road block."

I lifted my binoculars. "Hmm, we won't get past it. There's a barrier across the track. See, there're three elderly women sitting in lawn chairs to the right, and they have shotguns." What I didn't point out was that the old dears were as fat as butter.

"Oh shit," muttered Harold. He was biting his fingernails again.

"We've got to go now. There's no second chance." I grabbed him by the shoulders for effect, "They're as cunning as feral cats, so, this is your chance to shine. I've got a plan. Listen-up."

* * *

I made my way on foot to the ridgeline to our left and descended the other side using the gum trees and scrub for cover. When I was within throwing distance, I started lobbying the stone laden cans to my side of the barricade. They made a lot of commotion as they landed and rolled down the hill. The aging women stood and ran the best they could toward the landing spot. They were hollering and shouting, pointing their weapons.

I threw a few further along, drawing the women away from the roadblock. Then, on cue, Harold appeared over the crest, driving straight for the barricade. The women saw what was happening, turned around then ran back. By this time the old girls were tired from jogging. Nevertheless, they seemed determined to stop him and gave chase, their long skirts flapping the way flags do.

Harold turned his ute before he reached the barricade and drew them up the hill away from me. He slowed so they could gain on him, then he'd sped up slightly, leading them into the distance.

As if they were a squad of soldiers forming a skirmish line, they stopped, drew their shotguns. One of the women's barrels flamed. Another gun barked in anger. And the third gun blazed as the volley of shot pelted Harold's vehicle. They reloaded their single-barreled guns for a second barrage, and the landscape was alight with more muzzle flashes.

Over the radio I could hear Harold shouting, "Unreal! I'm taking Delta Hotel."

He was using military code for 'direct hits.' Harold must have thought it was a commando operation, something he never thought he'd be able to do. He was enjoying it. I was sure his hair was standing up without the aid of gel.

He was being immensely brave to have volunteered not knowing it was all an elaborate bluff on the part of the women. Nevertheless, I'm sure he could feel each shot as it connected with his *ute*.

By this time, I was in back my Holden racing down the track straight for the wooden shafts that lay across the track. At the last second, I swerved around the barricade, and was immediately heading up the hill on the other side. I had cleared the roadblock.

"Zulu Bravo, this is Zulu Prime."

"Prime, send."

"I'm on the move. Thanks." I knew it was unsporting to give the old girls moving targets, but I needed to get on with this. If my plan worked, Harold would be doubling back to the main track that we came down. I had instructed him to wait for me off the trail a few kilometers outside Copley and to monitor the frequency.

I was on my own. Finally! The only company I had now was a GPS with the coordinates Harold had programmed into it. If he did his job, it would lead me to Goat Canyon.

Twenty-Four

G oat Canyon was a rocky outcrop surrounded by a creek that forked around it, a sort of island with a steep slope leading to the top. The other three sides were cliffs forming a canyon.

I parked my vehicle facing the track from which I came, then I crossed the dry stony creek bed and took up a position at the base of the hill where I had a clear sight to Kurt's camp at the peak. His bivouac was on the left side near the end of the cliff that overlooked one of the branches in the creek.

Through my binoculars, I could see it consisted of a two-person tent and a small pile of rocks that appeared to be a fire ring for cooking. There was an artist's easel, holding a canvas with a depiction of an Aboriginal woman—*a basic camp, even for Boy Scout standards.*

Around the perimeter was a dozen of tall wooden poles fashioned from tree branches. On top of each was a severed goat's head. *Hmm, animal rights activists would do more than paint his door red if they saw this.* I snapped a few photos with my smartphone.

I could taste the rain coming. Made me impatient. The flaps of the tent opened, and an Aboriginal woman emerged. She was bare-chested and wore an amulet on a chain around her neck. I wondered if it was to ward off an evil spirit. Who knows which one? Perhaps the Commissioner of Internal Revenue.

She sauntered to a horse tethered just within sight. She walked as if she was floating, mounted the horse, then glanced back at the tent. After riding down the hill, she crossed the creek further to my right.

My mind drifted back to when I used to conduct stakeouts as a new PI. Fidelity investigations. After a few, I didn't do it anymore. I could never come away without being abused. If I didn't find the cheating partner, I was accused of being incompetent. If I did and got photos of the duplicitous partner, I'd cop a verbal beating for breaking the news.

Nevertheless, I snapped photos of her.

A moment later, Kurt emerged without a shirt and was pulling up his trousers, doing up his fly and belt. He was the image of the man in the photo in my dossier, only tired, unshaven, and seedy. *So, that's Kurt Kerslake.*

I took a few shots of him dressing.

The sky to the west was growing dark. A few drops of rain fell. Time to move.

I crossed the parched creek and started up the hill, weaving behind trees as I made a rapid approach. I wanted to maintain invisibility until the last minute.

Had no idea about how delusional he was but wasn't going to chance that my head would end up impaled like the goats. "Kurt Kerslake?"

He spun around to face me. "Who are you?"

"I'm a reporter with the *Wyoming County News*. I'm here to do a story about rocks."

"A story about *rocks*?" He shook his head.

I stepped closer.

He raised his voice as he said, "You come alone?"

"No, I've brought the Sydney Girls' Choir."

He grimaced and pointed a finger at me. "Why are you here?"

I looked around the camp, sized-up what was going on. Surreptitiously, I captured a few photos. "Because I want to sit around your campfire, toast marshmallows, and sing Kumbaya."

His eyes widened. "That's not true."

"What are you doing out here?" I asked without disguising my bewilderment.

He staggered, almost losing his balance. With Carrollian logic, he explained, "This is the promised land for the world's Indigenous peoples."

"This isn't your land. It belongs to another tribe. You need to come with me. You need rehab."

He put on his shirt and waved his hand at me as if he were trying to discourage a fly from landing. "So, my wife sent you. Well, tell her that society needs to put itself through *moral* rehab the way Germany did after the Second World War, and South Africa did after apartheid."

There was a sound of distant thunder that didn't ease my tension. I was in no mood for him to be my social worker. "Hey, whatever world you created in your head, you've got to leave now! Get your gear. Let's go!"

He regarded me as if I was a lump of dung. "What're you, some low-rent, dime-detective my wife hired?"

"Not a detective. An investigator. Cops are dicks. Privates are investigators."

I didn't dare tell him how much his wife was paying. It certainly wasn't nickels or dimes.

His face began to twitch. "How'd you find me?"

"You're hardly a ghost. You thrashed around, leaving your footprints everywhere." I swung my arm in an arc across his campsite. "Your Indigenous brothers would be horrified to see your lack of woodsmen skills."

He chuckled, quaffed from a plastic bottle that was at his feet then began a rant about caves and tunnels, systems of interconnecting burrows that traversed the earth's mantle. He said he didn't need to know bushcraft because living at the earth's core would provide everything. It would protect people from pollutants and rays emitted from the sun, such as solar flares that produced x-rays and UV radiation. He said the land at the center of the earth was inhabited by herds of mammoths shepherded by the descendants of ancient tribes. His people. That's why he was in Australia.

"The idea came to him while painting. He had a vision that told him the tunnel entrance was in Australia, and that it would allow him to descend into Paradise. The goats were a sacrifice to the leaders of the tribes. He said the cave dwellers were preparing to greet him then guide him to earth's center. "It's a world of perfect social harmony," he declared.

I recalled reading about people who believed in a Hollow Earth theory. A form of religion. I thought back to what Jack Perotti said about people's worship. *It gives them hope*.

"You know, if the animal liberationists ever find out what you've done here, they'll do more than spray paint a few slogans on your studio wall."

He didn't hear me. He was still raving on about how the U.S. government had used *Photoshop* to alter satellite images of this part of the earth to cover up the tunnel's entrance, but *he* was going to find it.

"They've put special electronic devices around the tunnel's entrance to jam GPS signals to prevent us from locating it," he ranted.

Seemed as though he'd slipped into a trance; was having a nightmare; talking in his sleep, or speaking in religious tongues, but he wasn't. It was his defective brain cells. He'd gone mad.

I couldn't tell if he was this way before he got here, or because he was here. I was sure it was connected to either the alcoholic demons that took refuge inside the dark places of his mind or the hallucinogenic drugs he took.

He said he had a CB radio that was immune to the effects of secret government agents. When he arrived at the center of the earth, he was going to set up a new World Government that would eliminate all other governments.

Then his speech began to slur, his lips didn't seem to work, and his eyes almost rolled back in his head. He went limp, like a doll, melting into a pile where he stood.

I reached for his pulse. Faint, but it was there. I searched for his medication, thinking maybe he'd gone into an insulin shock, or whatever Corey said about diabetics. My gaze shifted to a bottle by his feet. There was no label.

I picked it up. Smelled unpleasant. Perhaps it hadn't been decanted long enough, but I suspected it was some form of industrial alcohol.

At that moment, there was a blaze of lightning overhead. Thunder echoed around the canyon.

Oh, shit! He must have drunk this in desperation. I wondered if this stuff fueled his cauldron of hollow thoughts. Regardless, I had to get him out of there or neither of us would survive the rising water.

His camp was a remnant of a carnival of twisted ideas. If anyone ever discovered what he was doing out here, no one would buy his work in *any* gallery. No serious collector would be interested in the ravings of some psychedelic-crazed, alcoholic artist obsessed with bizarre dreams that included animal sacrifice.

Lying in a heap with urine stains around his crotch, his face took on the appearance of a deep-sea diver who'd surfaced without the aid of a decompression chamber.

Then I heard the trees straining against the wind, groaning as if they were in pain.

The likelihood the police would have to get involved was growing as his condition deteriorated. I knew what the ramifications of that would mean for Yvette.

The rain started to fall. Hard. I surveyed the site. It was difficult to see how Kurt could have enlarged Leon's mind. Hard to believe he was an oracle. Leon and his mates were apparently hoping for a miracle, but all they got was a mirage. Kurt's late-night radio listeners would have been better off listening to an audio book of Jules Verne's *The Underground City*. At least, that had a believable plot.

Kurt stirred and muttered several incoherent strings of words about Indigenous genocide at the hands of the U.S. government, purveyors of indiscriminate violence against his people, the extinction of countless Indigenous American languages.

The mind was powerful. Not only can it problem-solve—quantum mechanics, laser physics, the medical marvels that are awarded Nobel Prizes—but it can drive people to do things beyond what they'd see themselves doing—heroic feats. It also holds people back, inflicting paralyzing phobias, imagined fears, anxieties, and emotional upsets.

As he mumbled his soliloquy, I could see how his thinking had turned in on itself, making him sick rather than strong, creating demons rather than angels. In any case, I was witnessing a man who had created another world in his head, a place where he had moved in, permanently.

I grabbed his arm and lifted him to his feet. Rain dripped down his face. "Have you finished feeling sorry for yourself?"

He had the same stare as the impaled goats.

I shook him. "Listen. You can't drown your demons in alcohol. They know how to swim."

He looked like he was deep inside his closet of nightmares. I pictured his mind as a helium balloon. I needed to get a grip on his string otherwise he'd drift through the atmosphere in whatever direction took his fancy.

I needed to get him moving and would have prayed to anyone's God if I thought it would do any good. Then, a germ of an idea formed. In a flash, it came to me.

However, there was some cleaning-up I needed to do first...

Twenty-Five

"Hey, remember the big oil spill in the Gulf of Mexico?" I asked. "People forgot about it. Why? Because the intelligence agencies are mining all our personal information and using it to target our brains." I shook him. "Listen, Kurt; you're the victim of government mind control. People don't realize there are shadowy agencies out there manipulating people's thoughts. You need help to fight them. I know how to deflect their psychotronic control. What you need is an aluminum foil deflector beanie. You need to get out of here before it's too late."

His eyes brightened at my ridiculous suggestion. "Yes, before they discover I know about Hollow Earth."

Despite him having his arm around my shoulder, his feet behaved as if they were streamers in a gale. He couldn't keep one foot in front of the other and was throwing me off balance. I grabbed tighter, but nothing about him was hard. His whole body was rubbery.

The stench of rancid animal grease wafted from the foil cap I fashioned from what was around the campfire. So, when he lost consciousness, I swiped it off. At that stage, I slung him over my shoulders in a firefighter's carry; his weight propelled me down the hill. I stepped into the creek. The previous dry creek was flowing from the downpour. The water was cutting a swathe through the landscape and was moving fast, but only above my ankles. I hated the feel of water squelching in my boots, but I fought the need to rest. It was difficult walking with him on my shoulders. His pudgy form clung to me the way mud stuck to a shoe.

As the rain increased, the water whooshed past. I was mid-stream when I felt a plastic bag wrap around my leg. I cursed the camper who'd left plastic behind. I couldn't reach down to free myself of it, so I pressed on.

Then the bag moved. I thought it odd, but the wind was strong, so I didn't give it any more notice. Until it moved up my leg.

I was balancing on a large submerged stone. Dipping my gaze, I allowed my eyes to focus on my right leg.

A brown snake, its head about level with my knee, was trying to keep out of the water. I'm sure the late Steve Erwin would have casually reached down, grabbed the critter by the head, then whipped it over his shoulder.

Erwin, I was not. As the blood drained from my head, my peripheral vision started to disappear. Then, as if played in slow motion, I fell face-first into the flooded creek. Kurt's weight on my back pressed me under.

The sensation of water going down my throat immediately revived me. Gagging and coughing, I planted my feet on the stony creek bottom and thrust my torso into the air. The snake was gone, but so was Kurt. Sucking in a quick breath, I looked downstream. I swayed as I ran waist-deep with the current, searching for him.

Then I saw him. His body was lodged against the branches of a dead tree that was stuck in the stream. His head was upright but tilting at an acute angle.

Being pushed along by the deluge, I reached him in seconds. I knelt, slung his arm over my shoulder, and hoisted him onto my back. I wasn't sure if he was dead or alive, but I knew we'd both perish if I didn't get us out of that creek.

Resembling a bobber on a fishing line, I went up and down with the rush of water.

Once at the vehicle, I let Kurt's body slide off my shoulders and onto the passenger's seat. His head rolled back, and there was a groan. I slammed the door, reached through the open window, and grabbed his matted black hair then dragged him toward me. With his head out the window, he vomited. It reeked. What he heaved had the appearance of creek water, but with that factory alcohol smell. Nothing substantial came up.

There was more thunder. Shadows cast by the dark blue lightning flashes danced as I revved the engine and speed shifted through the gears. His sour breath clogged my nostrils as the rain pelted the vehicle.

Twenty-Six

"Zulu Bravo. Copy?"

I heard some static, then Harold Brigg's voice. "Send."

I pushed the transmit button. "The package is about to be delivered. Drop the owner at the intersection where the rail line crosses the dirt track on the outskirts of town. I'll deliver it there."

"Roger," came his reply.

"Tell the owner it's damaged. She needs to bring the *stuff* to repair it. After the drop-off, return to the RV."

I released to the button and heard only static.

Then came his reply, "Roger. Out."

Now and again I stole a glance at Kurt, but my mind was on keeping at least two wheels on the track as we headed back to Copley. I hoped the sobriety patrol would go for shelter, so I could slip around the barricade without incident. When I got there, it was a clear run as I'd anticipated.

I turned the Holden back toward the township. Kurt's face was as lifeless as one of Madame Tussaud's mannequins. When he opened his eyes, they took on the dull yellowish color of a cheap tawny port.

Then he made an unnatural guttural sound that came from deep within. "The rain is the heavens crying for me." His eyes were puffy as if he had been in a fight and wasn't the winner. "My words will be a clarion call to the world."

Cobalt lightning flashed in front of us.

Then he muttered, "The horror. The horror."

I suspected politics allowed him to see the world for the first time. The problem with seeing it is that it's hard to close your eyes once they have been opened, without a bit of help. In his case, that came from drinking. He had nothing to live for but distorted ideals. In the end, only darkness prevailed.

I reached across the cab, searched for a pulse. There was none. His head hung down, chin resting on his chest. I touched his wrist again, but like the waters of a dark pond, his thoughts now ran still and silent. He had cast his last dream, but unfortunately for him, the tide was out.

I was powerless to intervene, like when I watched Ellen die. I recalled how I held her in my arms, trying to press my life spirit into her to prevent her from slipping away. All the things she did in her life were gone. Her as a little girl, growing up in Scotland. Her first job, her university career, field research, publishing, marrying, kids, then death.

I didn't know much about Kurt other than the bits I gleaned from my background investigation and what Yvette told me. I had no idea who he was. All I knew was that people died every day. When they did, all they took with them and left behind was their memories.

What was I going to tell Yvette?

My training was to report the facts.

* * *

Ahead, standing on the side of the track outside Copley was Yvette. She had her R.M. Williams boots on, tight jeans, and a light tan leather jacket. It was still a bit windy, but the storm had passed as fast as it had descended.

Before I came to a stop, she had the back door open and flung herself in. She reached across the seat in front of her and hugged his lifeless body.

With lips trembling and through a shuddering voice, she asked, "What happened?"

I explained, handed her my smartphone, and while she stroked his lifeless head with one hand, she scrolled through the photos with the other.

Her green eyes showed fright, helplessness. She was alone in a forbidding place. Holding the phone with those photos appeared to give form to all her fears. It was as though she was Emperor Honorius watching the Visigoths coming over the seventh hill. I suspected she knew from the photos her empire was about to fall.

She searched my eyes deeply, for what seemed forever.

Instinct told me to drive to the Leigh Creek Hospital and let the medical examination process take its course. That could mean ruin for Yvette, and for Kurt's memory.

If I lied and was discovered, it would mean revocation of my PI license. Although the fate of the universe didn't depend on my decision, it was a serious conundrum.

I tightened my fists around the steering wheel, gave Yvette a nod, then said, "My instructions were no police, no lawyers."

Her eyes brightened.

I informed her, "There's no evidence. Everything you see in those photos is gone." And with a couple of taps on my phone, I deleted the pictures. A couple of more taps and I'd reformatted the phone, taking the internal memory back to its factory settings.

"I don't understand. How'd his camp disappear?"

"PIs preserve evidence and present it in court. Don't you think I know how to un-preserve it? I'm only a pseudo-Greenie, so I let the creek—that flood—take care of everything. Nothing from his camp will survive. Not even twenty FBI special agents could piece it together, and certainly, not Detective Sergeant Miller and that band of SES rescuers."

140

"What about your 'man in Havana'?"

"Never got near the place. Hasn't seen Kurt. That's why I got him to drop you here." I stared at her. "As soon as we arrive at the hospital, it's going to be as busy as Boston Common. It's your call. What do you want to do?"

She started to rock the way a monk does in prayer. If she was hoping for a miracle, I doubted any divine spirit could deliver that now.

Then she stopped. As if she was a Marine facing overwhelming odds, she appeared to be on the verge of taking the initiative, seizing the moment, improvising to overcome. As a spot of blue sky materialized on the horizon, something formed in her eyes: hope. She muttered something about the American Indian philosophy on death.

I started the vehicle. I could tell she was about to do something bold.

* * *

I followed the voice instructions given by the GPS, which led me to a sign-posted 'Leigh Creek Health Service.' I parked in the disabled car park near the front door and made a show of running inside.

"He's had a heart attack," I said, trying to sound more concerned than I was, feigning being out of breath. "In my car on the way here. Quick, he's outside."

The duty nurse grabbed her mobile phone and appeared to be speed-dialing someone.

When we got to the car, she tried for a pulse. As I knew, there was none. His color and general disposition must have told her he was beyond resuscitating. She swallowed as if she was unsure of what to say.

She left then came back with another nurse and an orderly with a stretcher. She said the doctor was on his way. "He'll need to examine him."

Doctor Huong Tran arrived in the emergency room. He was young. With a hint of a Vietnamese accent, he said how sorry he was for our loss. He asked Yvette if she was the next of kin and what happened.

"He had a heart attack. He's had minor attacks before and has been under the treatment of Professor Northrop Adams. You know, the head of cardiac research at Massachusetts General Hospital." She held up a small bottle of pills and shook them. "He should have been taking these but hasn't been conscientious since he's been on vacation."

"So, you are on vacation? From the States?"

"Yes, Kurt's an artist. An American Indian painter. He was here studying Aboriginal rock art techniques."

I heard echoes of the words she used to describe Mrs Walkley's paintings roll out of Yvette's mouth.

"He's filthy. What happened?"

I said, "He went for a walk. For inspiration. He got caught in the storm. I went to find him. He was complaining of tightness in his chest, shooting pains down his left arm. I thought it was serious, so I collected Yvette, and we drove here." I looked down for affect. "I wasn't quick enough." I reached for Yvette's hand to dramatize my words. I didn't say anything about him being a fall-down drunk with cirrhosis of the liver, or him so desperate for a drink that he drank poison, the things I should have said. Lifting my gaze, I said, "He was a remarkable man."

The doctor crossed his arms. "And who are you?"

"I'm his friend."

"There'll have to be an autopsy. I know nothing of his medical condition."

With a smile so warm it could melt a tray of ice-cubes, Yvette Kerslake said, "I don't think that'll be necessary, Doctor. This is too traumatic for me as it is." She caressed his arm. "I want to take him home as soon as possible. You see, as an American Indian, his spirit needs to return where it belongs, where his ancestors are." She handed him her phone.

He hesitated. "What's this?"

"Professor Northrop Adams is on the line. I phoned him. He'll sign the death certificate."

Doctor Tran took the phone, but as he went to hold it, she wrapped her hands around his and whispered, "After you speak to Professor Adams, I think you'll find that he might be interested in taking on a new registrar at Mass General. I'm sure that would be more agreeable to you than sticking out your residency here."

Whatever I thought her reaction might be when confronted by these medical people, I was wrong. She was as soothing as a balm. Maybe there was something in her words about death and the Truth it brings, or, it could have been she was *alluring and very complex.*

While Doctor Huong Tran talked into the phone, I lowered my voice, "How'd you do that?"

"My father will simply make a little larger than normal contribution to the professor's research fund."

Doctor Tran mumbled some medical terms, exchanged a few words of thanks, and ended with, "Okay Professor, I'll await your email." He faced us. "No need for an autopsy, Professor Adams will take care of the paperwork. He's familiar with Mr Kerslake's condition. I'll organize for the U.S. Consulate to help you repatriate Mr Kerslake from the emergency landing strip in the morning. Mrs Kerslake, you'll be more comfortable in the Leigh Creek Hotel. I'll organize for your bags to be brought there."

Doctor Tran tilted his head at me. "I'll book two rooms. Sorry, Mr.— I didn't catch your name."

I stuck my hand out; we shook. I introduced myself. "Thanks, but I'll be staying in Copley for a while. I have a friend who lives in town."

"As you choose." Then he left us alone.

"What friend? That girl from the plane?" asked Yvette.

"Yeah."

With an impatient huff, she said, "Yeah? No explanation?"

My job was finished. I did what I set out to do. This was my personal life. I dodged the question. "If I stay long enough, I won't have to worry about fitting snow tires to my jeep."

She shook her head. "Send me your bill. I'm happy to pay."

"What you paid already is satisfactory."

"I can be more generous. By the time Kurt is buried, his paintings will have quadrupled in price. His paintings evoke power and depth of emotion."

I thought about Kurt's painting of the Aboriginal woman I threw into the creek.

"The three galleries that had been discussing whether they'd buy more of his work will purchase everything he has stored in his studio. Death brings a limited supply. Limited supply means the highest price. It's pure market forces."

I mused about my friend Lucian and his global lecture circuit, wondering if she had heard him give his talk about 'the bottom-line.'

She touched me with the same gentleness she gave the registrar. "I'll add on a bonus. For the *discreet* service."

Her offer made me feel unprincipled. I could have been insulted, but I wasn't that proud. We all do what we need to do

144

to get through life. I did what I did to help her through her storm. Kurt was dead. He'd caused her misery. She waited for him to give her a child, waiting for a ship she thought was somewhere over the horizon.

Any day now, I'm sure she kept telling herself. Nevertheless, that ship never came. How wrong I was when we met to think she might have been ill-treating him. She wasn't a woman I could relate to, but she was human, and she had to get through the rest of her days carrying the burden she'd just inherited.

I smiled. "Thanks. You have my bank details. I'll leave it for you to decide."

Twenty-Seven

I swung the nose of the Holden into a vacant park in front of the pub. This was our RV. There were only a few vehicles, but I could see Harold sitting in his *ute*. No doubt he was still monitoring the radio scanner.

"Hey, did you go for a swim in that creek," he asked, poking fun at me.

"Yeah."

"Wonder if you saw any crocs?"

"No, the sharks scared them away."

He gave a booming laugh. "What happened?"

"Doc says it was a heart attack."

"Sorry to hear. She okay?"

"She'll be fine."

With sincerity in his voice, he said, "I want to thank you for what you did for me. The opportunity, I mean. No one has ever included me in anything like that before."

His words made me proud. Facing those shotguns was a mighty feat. Believing that there was lead shot in those blasts would've made most men break out in a cold sweat. In his case, it elevated his inner strength.

I stuck out my hand. "Well, I'd thank you for your help, but because the mission never existed, I can't."

He glowed as he squeezed my hand with zest. "Roger that! I suppose your work is finished. Heading home?"

"No, Mrs Kerslake will be taking her husband's body home tomorrow morning. I'll be staying on, with my—" I cleared my throat. "—with my girlfriend."

"Wow, you work fast."

"Maybe I'll see you back here for a drink tonight." I paused when I glanced over his shoulder. "On second thought, looks as though Viktor Gjeka's mates are over there. Must be waiting for him. Perhaps we should steer clear of this place."

His two goonish friends were sitting on the hood of their light truck drinking beer from cans.

"I'm not going to let them push me around anymore."

"Hey, don't do anything stupid. That's why we have politicians. Let me check out. I'll get my gear and see you here in a few minutes."

I saw Carrie, paid my bill, then went upstairs to collect my duffle bag. On the way down, I heard a man screaming in agony.

Harold? What's he done?

I leapt two steps at a time, jumped the last four, then pushed open the door to the street. I saw Harold. He had one hand on Viktor's backside, the other grabbing his collar. He was frog marching him out the pub's door.

Gjeka landed face first in the mud and skidded to a stop. He rolled over, yelling, "You broke my fucking hand! Busted my bloody arm!"

His friends rushed over, stood him up, then walked him to their truck.

"Get him a bucket of cement. He needs to toughen up," taunted Harold.

Over his shoulder, Gjeka bellowed, "I'll come looking for you!"

With his hands on his hips, Harold said, "Come. I won't be hiding."

"Hey, I was only gone a few minutes. What happened?" I asked.

He said, "I heard Carrie shouting for him to get out. I went in. Gjeka was telling her that women were only good for one thing—providing something soft to lie on while having sex. I remembered what you said—appeasement never works—so I told him to shut his mouth and get out. He took a swing at me. I ducked. He smacked the wall. The rest you saw." He winked at me. "I think Carrie will see me in a different light."

I gave him the thumbs up. "I think you'll be disappointed to find out that Viktor's going to de-friend you on social media."

* * *

I pulled the Holden over to the side of the gravel road that crossed the train line. I cast my gaze across the skyline. My limbs went loose. I was content; no need to fill the silence. It was a moment of clarity. In that instant, I realized I was about to make the wrong decision. Memories whorled around in my head like a carousel that was out of control. I needed to do something different.

After turning off the engine, I dialed Sophie. Her line rang several times then switched to her message service. I disconnected. It was early in the morning for her, so I figured she'd be driving to work. I tapped out a message explaining what I had in mind and pressed the send key.

The wind had died. There were only one or two clouds about. The setting sun's rays struck the landscape, the azure sky throwing long, colorful shadows that had warmth.

My phone chimed. Sophie. My message must have sparked her attention.

"I'm glad you told me what you're thinking because I need to explain a few things," she said. "You'll never figure it out on your own." Then with her hallmark drawn-out inflection, she said, "If you don't do as I say, I'll hate you forever."

She then gave me her advice...

* * *

We sat on her front veranda nestled between the arms of her two-seater sofa. Faye Bellcroft wore a tapered, white embroidered linen blouse. I was covered in dried creek mud. She was sweet-scented. I needed a shower.

Barney laid on a damp patch of ground near the gate. He didn't seem to mind.

"You're such a pleasant change from the blokes who work in the music industry. They think because they see you in the dressing room in your bra, you'll fall for their pick-up lines."

From the distance, I could hear the approach of the coal train. It was starting its long haul from the mine site to the Port Augusta power station, about a five-hour trip to the south.

"Thanks, but no matter how big they build aircraft, or how fast they fly, the east coast of the States will always be on the other side of the world," I pointed out.

With rawness in her voice, she put it to me, "We're too old to be coy. I feel it. I need to know whether you feel it too."

A lizard wandered across her front yard. Its body shifted from side-to-side in a choreographed display of slow motion, but my heart pounded at 160. I didn't know what was worse— trying to marshal the nerve to say it or face Sophie if I didn't. "I'll be honest with you. I won't lie. You're *not* a close friend to me."

Her lips quivered. She blew out a short breath. I couldn't see the color of her eyes—they were glazed with mist.

With the last rays of the day dancing on Barney's back, I thought about the new cards I had drawn from the deck at the table-of-life. They were the result of a stroke of fortune. I looked around. Although there weren't the autumn leaves in the sun-dappled woods of back home, I was convinced that this was a garden where I could flourish.

Becoming dew-eyed myself, I managed to say, "Because I want you to be my fiancée. I love you."

149

Faye squeezed her eyebrows together as she focused. "Are you asking me? I've never been asked." A mischievous smile appeared on her face. "Except by blokes who had far too much to drink."

Before I could say anything, she added, "You won't regret asking, if that's what you're going to do." She flickered her gaze. "I'm completely in love with you."

The dam holding back my tears burst. They streaked down my face in a parade of joy.

I reached into my pocket and pulled out my old wedding ring. "I'm sorry, I didn't have time, but would you accept this as a promissory until I can get you a proper one?"

Her linen blouse brushed my skin as we hugged. The sweet smell of her floral fragrance wrapped around me. I had the premonition that this was going to be a wonderful garden.

- o O o -

About the Author

Oliver Yardley is a pseudonym for a former Australian government intelligence officer and freelance private investigator who spent his career in various operational fields, including security, investigation, and counterterrorism. He also served for over a decade as a research criminologist at Charles Sturt University, Sydney, specializing in the study of transnational crime—espionage, terrorism, drugs and arms trafficking, and cyber-crime. In addition to his BSc, MSocSc, and PhD degrees in criminology, he holds an MPhil in English literary theory.